FROM THE SUNDERING SNOWS

SNOWS

AN ILBEOR STORY

T.J. KLAPPRODT

This book is a work of fiction. Names, characters, businesses, events, and incidents are the products of the author's imagination. Any resemblance to actual persons, living or dead, or actual events is purely coincidental.

This work and its cover art was wholly composed by human creators. No generative AI was used.

Copyright 2024 T.J. Klapprodt

All rights reserved. No part of this book may be reproduced or used in any manner without the prior written permission of the copyright owner, except for the use of brief quotations in a book review.

To request permissions, contact the author at tj@tjklapprodt.com

Paperback: 979-8-9898905-4-5
eBook: 979-8-9898905-3-8

First Edition: July 2024

Cover Art by GetCovers.com

To Alan, a genius of storytelling and fantasy, who has been with me on this journey from the start. None of this would have been possible without him.

SHAAMEL

early a thousand years...it had been nearly a thousand years, and he still could not tear his eyes away from her beauty.

Aenwyn lay sleeping in the predawn hours, her luscious golden red hair fanned across the feather pillow, her face peaceful and relaxed, and her small mouth open ever so slightly as she breathed steadily and evenly. Altoneir wanted to kiss her, wanted to just lean over and kiss that smooth, lightly pink cheek, but he didn't want to wake her. Not yet; not when the business of the day had not begun.

He smiled softly, watching her chest rise and fall, the fabric of her blue silken nightgown seeming to shimmer with the movement. The sight was as familiar to him as the home they had inhabited for over five hundred years, the home that reflected who they were as surely as anything else did.

Altoneir glanced around the large space that comprised the main room of the round, thatched-roof dwelling so similar to the many others in their settlement. The walls, white and smooth by both age and design, were lined with small alcoves, each of which held a flickering elven light not yet extinguished in the hours of the predawn. He had always enjoyed the way those lights favored Aenwyn's pale skin;

even now, as she lay sleeping, one from just over their bed cast a soothing yellow glow over her face. They had chosen every piece of furniture, every accoutrement and knickknack, with such care that he felt their home exuded both their personalities; for Aenwyn, delicate blown glass figurines made by the dwarves offered calming blues and greens to the space; for Altoneir, sturdy but intricately carved furniture of dark wood reflected his eye for detail and beauty in the artistic.

Altoneir thought of the stone he had received from the dwarf miners who had visited with their wares just before the winter had struck in earnest. Though the season had progressed through the winter and into early spring, he still hadn't touched it, hadn't attempted to fit it into a setting for wear. Now, though, he thought of both those things.

He would take the beautiful cut diamond he had bought on a whim, and he would set it in the finest silver. He would set it, and then he would place it on a fine silver chain at the perfect length to fall just above the cleft of her breasts. For truly, who else could that diamond have been meant for if not his beloved Aenwyn?

As though she sensed his attention, Aenwyn stirred, slowly turning to face him. Altoneir noticed a tangle in her long hair, as often happened when she slept, and he reached out to gently comb his long fingers through it until the strands rested with the rest of her silken tresses.

She smiled sleepily. "Best of the morning to you, lover," she said softly. "Is it yet sunrise?"

He smiled back at her, his face full of the tenderness they had shared for almost a millennium. She asked that question every morning, and every morning his answer was the same. "No, my love. It is but predawn and the world has yet to stir from its sleep."

She reached out a hand to stroke his cheek, running her fingers over the slight stubble he had not yet removed. He leaned into the touch, relishing her soft, cool fingers on his face.

"Shall we enter the world?" she asked after they had lain such for several minutes, simply looking at one another, sharing soft touches. It was their favorite way to greet the day.

"Yes, my beloved. Yes."

~

AYDUIN AND NALAEA, ancient and wise but looking no older than they had millennia ago, sat at the large table in the front room of their roundhouse. Nalaea smiled fondly at her son and his mate, always satisfied to see the love and partnership radiating between the two of them. It mirrored how she felt about her own mate.

Ayduin also gazed at Altoneir and Aenwyn. His face didn't exhibit the same indulgent tenderness as his mate's, but neither was it unkind. "The building of a family hall in Shaamel is long overdue," he said. "Though your mother and I enjoy our own dwelling, even as I am certain you enjoy yours, the family always dwelled in a family hall prior to our move here. It was such in Aidawyra before the Crossing, and it was such in Y'Sathemar. Only an overabundance of caution and resistance to the change has caused us to go centuries here after the treaty without building a new one."

Before Altoneir could answer his father, Aenwyn smiled at him. She had always had a soft spot for Ayduin, despite his serious manner and lack of open affection. "*Apa*," she said, addressing him as she had since she and Altoneir had mated, "neither your son nor I object to the building of a family hall. Though we enjoy our roundhouse, we would enjoy even more quarters which would allow us to commune with you, our parents and elders."

Ayduin smiled at her, and Altoneir wondered, as he often did, whether his father was aware of the carefully wrought flattery with which Aenwyn spoke to him. He thought Ayduin must be; to Altoneir, it seemed obvious. Aenwyn, he knew, had even more than the usual respect of the elven people for their elders - but it seemed to him she treated his father with special reverence. Not for the first time, he wondered why that was so.

As his father lifted his hand and caused a rolled scroll of thick parchment to float toward the table from the curved-back sideboard where it had been resting, Altoneir wasn't surprised by what he assumed were plans for the family hall. Ayduin was a silversmith by trade and seemed to enjoy that work, but his genuine passion lay in designing buildings and habitations within Shaamel, and before it, Y'Sathemar.

Y'Sathemar. As Altoneir waited for his father to unveil the design, he thought of the settlement in the valley of Ilbeor where he and Aenwyn, along with his parents, had lived before the ancients elves of Caalenor had treated with the newly arrived humans rather than to protect what had been theirs for so long. They had ceded the valley to the new race without consideration for those already living there, and the insistence that the elves of Y'Sathemar and other settlements in the valley move into the mountain ranges to the west had caused vast amounts of upset. Even now, several centuries later, even though they had been peacefully and fruitfully settled in Shaamel for so long, the forced departure from their previous home still rankled.

Ayduin unrolled the scroll by hand rather than with magic, presenting what was inside with an understated flourish of pride. Leaning in to gaze at the meticulously drawn design, Altoneir couldn't fault his father for being proud to show them what he had wrought. If built according to this design, the family hall would indeed be a building unlike any other in Shaamel.

Though the walls of the various rooms were rounded in homage to the elves' preference for their traditional roundhouses, the building itself was set in a more rectangular shape that allowed for a larger common area than was usually built, surrounded by spacious, rounded rooms that opened into it. The configuration of the rooms was like that of most other family halls, both in Shaamel and before its existence, but the rooms themselves, Altoneir could see, offered spectacular views of the mountainside and settlement.

Nalaea spoke, trailing an olive-toned finger along the edge of what would be Altoneir's and Aenwyn's private space, her white water-cloth robes trailing in the wake of the movement. "The entire wall opens," she said. "Your father has placed a new sort of hinge based upon his own design. When fully engaged, it will be as though the window-wall does not even exist, and your habitation will be open to the elements in fine weather. Is it not splendid?"

Aenwyn leaned in yet closer, inspecting the drawing with an appreciative eye. "I have never seen the like," she murmured, and Altoneir knew it wasn't flattery this time. Unlike himself and his parents, Aenwyn had been born in Ilbeor. Though over the millennia since the Crossing, the elves had built some spectacular structures, nothing compared to the grandeur of their former home. This design contained hints of that grandeur while still preserving the more understated style most of the elves of Ilbeor had adopted.

"Feast your eyes upon this room," Nalaea suggested, again trailing her fingernails along the edge of the design. Altoneir and Aenwyn both looked. Though perhaps smaller, it did not seem very different from the other rooms of the hall.

"What is it?" Aenwyn asked.

"It is the room," Ayduin said gravely, "reserved for your future offspring and, if they wish to stay, their future mate."

Altoneir and Aenwyn looked at one another, somehow feeling as though they had been reprimanded, though they knew that wasn't actually the case. "The fruit of my womb has not yet ripened, *Apa*," Aenwyn finally said. Though she and Altoneir had been fervently wishing for a child for over five hundred years, conception for elves came rarely and some mates waited more than a thousand years to conceive.

"I dreamed of your child," Nalaea said, as though this explained the implied question. "I believe you will conceive soon, daughter, and I believe you will have a daughter of your own."

Despite himself, Altoneir smiled. His mother was no prophet; her dreams had never been the foretelling kind. But to see the beautiful pink tinge bloom on Aenwyn's cheeks and hope kindle in her eyes as she once again allowed herself to dream of becoming a mother was to see the very sun rising before him.

Ayduin cleared his throat and changed the subject, announcing where in Shaamel he wished to build their family hall. And with that, the conversation shifted to less emotional subjects. By the time they rose to conduct their daily business, the light of hope in Aenwyn's eyes had faded, though her countenance remained as serene as it ever was.

~

"WHAT MATTERS WILL you attend this morning, Healer?" Altoneir asked as they strolled through Shaamel arm-in-arm in the crisp breeze of early spring. As always, their chosen robes presented a pleasing contrast: while Altoneir preferred earth tones and wore robes of light brown, Aenwyn wore robes of the brightest blue she had been able to find.

Aenwyn answered, "I have no pressing matters. I must check in on Rohana, of course." Rohana, a young woman by elven standards, had suffered a minor fall two days previously and was currently abed while her ankle healed.

"You have not been called urgently for some time," Altoneir commented. As a healer, there were times at which she was even called out of their bed for an emergency, but everything she had tended lately had been of a minor sort.

"Do not tempt fate," Aenwyn laughed. "I must gather herbs today, for the winter has depleted my stores, and it is time to bolster them."

As was their custom, they crossed Shaamel to Altoneir's shop first, where Aenwyn would leave him and depart to conduct her own business. As a master jewelcrafter, Altoneir spent his days bent over his worktable, creating the stunning pieces sought after throughout the elven and human communities of Ilbeor. Though he went about his work with the dogged determination of an elf serious about his trade, Aenwyn knew that the sparkling beauty of the gemstones he worked with had caught his attention since he was very young.

"Ah, Altoneir." The voice greeting him had a snide quality Altoneir immediately recognized as it sounded from behind them. "Aenwyn," the voice said more civilly.

Altoneir wanted nothing more than to walk away from the source of that voice, but courtesy demanded he turn and greet Paeral, the settlement's primary baker. Ambitious and always seeming to curry favor with the elders, Paeral grated on Altoneir's nerves, and it appeared the feeling was mutual.

"Good morning, Paeral," Altoneir said stiffly as he turned. "Should you not be plying your trade?"

"I could say the same of you."

Aenwyn stepped in before the situation could become heated, as it often did between the two males. "How does Inaadi fare this morning, Paeral?"

Paeral's face softened as he looked at her and spoke of his own mate. "Inaadi is well. She sets off for a spring hunt this afternoon, having had matters to attend with her parents this morning."

"Just as we did," Altoneir said. "My father is to build a family hall on the outskirts of the settlement." He felt no small measure of pride in announcing this news to his oftentimes rival.

"I suspect you will enjoy living in a more suitable situation, Aenwyn," Paeral said, his lip curling slightly.

"Our roundhouse is perfectly sufficient -" Altoneir began, color rising in his cheeks as he fell for the baited words.

"Of course it is," Paeral interrupted. "But for two such esteemed members of the settlement, I would have expected you to make improvements centuries ago. Do you truly enjoy living in such a small dwelling, Aenwyn?"

Though it was the second time Paeral had directly addressed his mate, Altoneir knew the comments were meant for him, to humiliate and condemn him for providing a home for his mate smaller and less lavishly adorned than many others in Shaamel. Preference rather than poverty or necessity had made the choice, but he knew it was a choice many in the settlement did not completely understand.

Before he could respond, Aenwyn again addressed the situation. "Size does not constitute a home, Paeral, nor do lavish adornments. Altoneir and I prefer living simply, and it is our preference that has led our roundhouse to remain unchanged over the years. Our home is with one another, regardless of if we dwell in a roundhouse, a family hall, or in a camp under the trees and stars." Her voice was gentle and light, but neither male missed the edge of remonstrance in her words.

Paeral had the grace to look abashed, and he addressed his response to Aenwyn with no hint of continuing to bait Altoneir. "My apologies, Healer," he said formally. "Of course, one should live as one prefers. I only meant to say I am certain Ayduin will build a family hall to rival the splendors of Caalenor, and I am happy you will have the pleasure of dwelling within it."

Aenwyn graciously inclined her head at him, but Altoneir was satisfied to note that she didn't absolve Paeral of responsibility for the snide words he had spoken.

Paeral waited for a moment, seemingly hoping she would speak those words to him. When neither Altoneir nor Aenwyn said anything further, his cheeks flushed, and he dipped his head at them. "Best of the morning," he mumbled before continuing on his way.

Altoneir and Aenwyn continued their stroll in the quiet companionship of long-time partners until they reached Altoneir's workshop, which also served as a small storefront for any Shaamel elves who wished to purchase his creations. Altoneir brightened as Aenwyn kissed him lightly, trailing her hand down his cheek in a loving caress before leaving him to attend to Rohana and gather her herbs.

As Altoneir entered the shop, both his mind and his eye immediately went to the small wooden box on his shelf containing the diamond he had purchased from the dwarves. As it often did, the design he wished to create around the stone flashed into his mind's eye all at once. His best creations were always conceived such; it was as though some force beyond himself guided his creative process and imposed upon his mind that which he was meant to create.

He had matters to attend to before beginning work and, closing the arched wooden door against the early spring chill, he bustled about the workshop to prepare for his day. As he always did, he kindled his fire first, using magic to ignite the kindling and logs he had placed in the stone fireplace the day before. He waited for the fire to become hot enough to make his usual cup of herbal tea, the concoction carefully wrought by Aenwyn to offer him clarity of thought and sight, alertness and focus. Even after centuries, she refused to tell him what herbs she included in the mix, only that he was the only one she made it for.

The worktable having been cleared and cleaned before he left, he had only to gather the supplies he would need for the day's work. By the time he had carefully arranged the materials, the box containing the diamond in pride of place in the middle, the fire was hot enough to boil his water for tea. Placing the kettle on the trivet made especially for that purpose, Altoneir continued his morning routine.

Two large windows set with clear elven glass provided ample light for his work and, in accordance with his routine, he stood in front of each one in turn, waving a hand across it. Though the windows were clean to begin with, the wordless magic removed any stray bits of dust or dirt from their surfaces. After going outside to attend to the other sides of the glass, the windows were so perfectly clear it would have been easy to imagine the glass not being present at all.

The kettle sitting over the fire behind him moved ever so slightly as the water within it came to a rolling boil; though its lack of stability might have been considered a fault to others, Altoncir rather enjoyed the merry rattle it created on the trivet.

His tea steeping in a white clay mug to his left side, Altoneir finally opened the box containing the dwarven diamond. For a moment he just stared at it, taking in every detail of its color, composition, and existing cut. It was truly a magnificent stone, one of the best he had ever seen in his thousands of years practicing his craft. The diamond contained no defects, which was a rare occurrence. About the size of his thumb from the top knuckle to his fingertip, the size lent itself well to a substantial setting and design without being so large as to be overwhelming or too heavy.

He leaned closer, examining the cut of the stone. The dwarven artist had cut more facets into the stone than was usual; it was not a style of cut he usually enjoyed, but he found in this case the reflection of light from the facets caused the jewel to sparkle in a way that resembled white fire.

Only after he was certain he had taken in every detail he could visually did Altoneir pluck the stone from its box and begin examining it by touch. A smile formed on his face as his fingers fairly tingled with the expectation of the work about to commence. After taking the first sip of his tea, Altoneir set to his task.

THOUGH NEITHER ALTONEIR nor Aenwyn could have explained what was different about their lovemaking that early spring afternoon, there was a marked change, nonetheless. Over the centuries, they had become as intimately familiar with one another's bodies as with their own, and though the pleasure in their coupling had never diminished, the actions and soft words, touches and thrusts, moans of pleasure and gasps of ecstasy had become a song and dance they knew as well as the beats of one another's hearts.

Aenwyn lay naked over the top of the coverlet, her cheeks again tinged pink and her breathing ragged as Altoneir traced a long finger down her sleek abdomen, dipping into her navel and back out again as they continued the journey downward.

"Are you ready, my heart?" As he spoke, he kissed her lower abdomen tenderly, the kiss containing all the hope they had for the child they wanted so desperately. The idea had come to him that morning while he had worked over the diamond; what if he were to cast a spell into Aenwyn's very womb, a spell that carried all the love he had for her, a spell that carried their hopes to bring life into the world?

Aenwyn, as a healer, had seemed dubious that such a spell could bring physical changes to her body, the changes needed to ripen her womb for childbearing, but she had agreed to let him try and had even supplied him with a simple healing spell meant to carry the emotive magic into her body.

"For our child," he whispered, raising his upper body so he could gaze into her eyes. Before she could respond to him with so much as a nod or a sigh, he passed a soft palm over her lower abdomen, where her womb lay hidden and ready to bear their child.

Aenwyn gasped as she felt the magic pass from his hands into her body. Though the spell should not have been in any way painful, Altoneir gazed at her with concern. He was more magically powerful than almost any elf in Ilbeor, but he was no healer. He suddenly felt as though he might have hurt her inadvertently, even though the intention of the spell had been to do anything but.

Her voice came out in a whisper that sounded almost awed. "I felt…a change pass through my womb. It felt enlivening, quickening, as though…as though I myself am no longer the same."

"Shhhh," he soothed her, leaning forward to kiss her softly on her full, pink lips. "I would never change any part of you." He knew the depths of his power and knowledge sometimes frightened others, and he was relieved to find he hadn't hurt her. As for the change she felt… he felt hopeful about it, as though perhaps the spell had indeed had the intended effect.

Their foreplay temporarily forgotten, Aenwyn propped herself up on her elbows and gazed at her mate with a rare seriousness. "My body is now prepared for a child, my love," she murmured. "Though nothing in my healing arts suggests this should be possible, I know in my heart that what you have done will bear the most beautiful fruit the world has ever seen."

"Magic works in mysterious ways, as you know better than most others," Altoneir said softly. "Perhaps…" His voice trailed off as he considered the possibilities; in truth, he had not expected his magic to have such an immediate or discernible effect.

After considering for a moment, Aenwyn nodded slowly and relaxed back onto the bed, only raising one hand in a caress from his forehead, trailing down his cheek and into the curve of his neck. Altoneir closed his eyes at the loving touch, the trusting touch, the hopeful touch she offered to him. After a quiet moment, his fingers resumed their exploration of her body and his lips again bestowed light kisses.

Their coupling that afternoon was slow and sweet, full of dreams they had not dared utter for centuries, and it seemed to Altoneir that with each thrust of his body, with each touch and each kiss, he acted for their child...a child that seemed more real now than ever in their past attempts. He even thought he might be feeling the effects of the magic himself as he moved inside her; he knew now what she had meant when she had told him something within her had changed.

As they pulled their bodies apart and lay together, their breathing somewhat ragged but content, he thought of the small seed he might have planted in her womb, and he viewed the future it implied with a happiness he could not describe.

ALTONEIR LEFT AENWYN SLEEPING, sated, on their bed as he dressed himself for his afternoon return to his workshop. Her work for the day was complete, but he had often found his most creative and productive time to be in the late afternoon, after their daily respite. With Aenwyn's diamond fixed firmly in his mind's eye, he enjoyed the brisk air of the early spring as he made the trek back to his shop.

By the time he had entered his workshop and taken care of the tasks needed for his afternoon work, Altoneir again took the white diamond into his long fingers. He had not had to make many adjustments to the cut; the many-faceted cut it had come to him with had pleased him in its original form.

Setting the diamond down on the velvet cushion inside its small box, Altoneir turned his attention to the silver setting he wished to use for the necklace. Ayduin had wrought the design with care, and like the diamond, Altoneir had kept the piece for later use. He smiled softly at the silver half-circlet that would form the top of the setting: Ayduin had formed the silver into a wreath of spring flowers, each so detailed it seemed to live through the gleaming, perfect silver. Large enough to provide a substantial setting but yet somehow still conveying a sense of the delicacy of new growth, it would be the perfect accompaniment to the extraordinary diamond.

After taking measurements of the diamond for the third time to ensure his accuracy, Altoneir began the silver work for the rest of the setting. Working over it meticulously, using small streams of his own magic to heat the metal when necessary, Altoneir became completely absorbed in his work, and with the absence of any visitors or customers, the setting was beginning to take form as the afternoon waned into early evening.

As Altonier arranged his worktable for the following day's labor, the first cry of alarm sounded from outside, seemingly from the higher end of Shaamel. He rushed out his door; cries of alarm from the serene community were so very rare he knew something must be sorely amiss. As he burst through the door and into the settlement, he saw the other shopkeepers and tradesmen doing the same. All of them looked around, at first not able to see the source of one of their citizens' distress.

Just as Altoneir was preparing to run to alert Aenwyn that someone likely needed her help as a healer, the first of the shopkeepers saw the danger and shouted, pointing up the mountain.

Two thousand years of life could never have prepared Altoneir for what he saw when he followed Valeth's gaze: a wall of snow racing down the mountain toward Shaamel, cleaving and burying everything in its path. Even as they all stared in horror, the avalanche reached the topmost building in Shaamel, a stone watchtower that had been one of the first structures constructed when they had founded the settlement.

The ancient stone structure, always considered a symbol of strength and safety, fell under the onslaught of snow as if it had been made of nothing more than straw.

Without another glance at the other elves or the destruction being wrought up the mountain, Altoneir turned and raced toward home.

STILLNESS

$\mathcal{I}$t came with a kind of inexorable majesty, flowing down the mountain in a curtain of ice and snow, its beauty belying its destructive force. As he sprinted toward home and Aenwyn, Altoneir noted that most of the other elves were seeking safety inside their homes or shops. Though he fervently hoped they would find sanctuary, after what the avalanche had done to the stone watchtower, he doubted the other buildings would provide adequate cover.

Forcing himself to slow in the slightest measure, Altoneir extended his hands as he ran, pointing at the roundhouses and shops along his route home. Without a word or incantation, he sent waves of magical fortification towards each of the structures, hoping the strengthening spells would provide some protection from the onslaught.

The avalanche reached him just as his home came into view. Aenwyn stood on the threshold, pale as death, her hand reaching toward him.

"Shield!" Altoneir shouted at her, flinging one last wave of his magic towards his very reason for living. With nothing left to be done and no time to physically reach her, all Altoneir could do was surround himself in the same bubble of protection he had attempted to cast on her and others.

The blow was like nothing he had ever experienced. Through his magical ties to the shield he had cast around himself, he could feel the strain of the hard cushion of air as it held against the onslaught. The shield, though it kept the snow from entombing him, did nothing to hold him steady against it. Altoneir felt himself tumbling faster than he'd ever moved, his body twisting and contorting until he could no longer determine not only which direction he was traveling, but which way the surface lay. Terror such as he had never felt utterly consumed him as the layers of snow extinguished the evening light entirely.

His tumble through pitch-black space was over in less than a minute, but the experience might have lasted days for the pain wracking his entire body and the terrifying, unending blackness enclosing him on all sides. He jolted to a stop with a jarring finality so complete that some part of his mind registered he must have hit something. As he slowly gathered his wits, the one thing…that most important thing in his entire world…crashed back into his consciousness with a force of the very avalanche that had decimated his world.

Aenwyn.

Aenwyn, whose magic was the gentle magic of the healer rather than the brute magic of the warrior. Aenwyn, who had never had cause to protect herself from any major danger in her entire peaceful existence. Aenwyn, who had been reaching for him as they were separated…

Altoneir struggled, his breathing turning ragged as hysteria overtook the calm reason of his two thousand years. The shield of hard air vanished as he lost his focus on the magic, but surprise registered even through the panic that the snow encasing him did not immediately cave in.

In his frantic effort to free himself, to find her, to save her, Altoneir didn't even think about using magic. He slammed the flat of his hand into the wall of white in front of him, not yet even aware which way he was pointed. He met solid resistance; the snow, rather than being the fluffy white he usually encountered during winter, was as hard and unyielding as stone.

The pain of the blow resonated through his hand, his wrist, and his lower arm to the elbow, but it also served as an instrument to cut through his blinding fear. Think…if he was to free himself, if he was to find her, he must *think*.

Forcing himself to calm his breathing and stop his frantic struggle, Altoneir evaluated his situation. The first thing he had to do was figure out which way he must dig to reach the surface of the snow. His position, which he had not taken the time to ascertain in the preceding moments, indicated that he was lying sideways, his head tilted slightly downward.

In the small space left by his absent shield, Altoneir righted himself. He knew that, though he possessed the physical strength to tunnel through the hard-packed snow, he might be buried several feet or even yards deep. Moments were precious in this situation; he would have to use magic, but in such a way as to not cause the makeshift cave surrounding him to collapse. If it did and he lost his freedom to move, he knew his life would be in danger and, thus, his ability to find his mate.

Calling to mind the same hyper-focused heat he used in jewel-crafting, he allowed a spear of reddish-orange light to shoot from his upturned palm and into the packed snow above him, the beam causing the space to glow as though it were on fire. He heard the sizzle of evaporating water before the new fissure began to drip on his head. Carefully, slowly, Altoneir maintained and widened the column of heat, carving his way gently and precisely upward until the beam broke the surface only about two feet over his head. The relief of the small beam of light and air now piercing its way into the darkness threatened to undo him as he forced himself to maintain his focus and work slowly, widening the fissure until he knew he could stand and free himself.

When his head broke the surface, he used a cushion of air again, this time to gently lift himself out with as little disturbance to the surrounding snow as possible. Free from his dark entombment, Altoneir gazed at what the wall of snow had left behind.

∼

STILLNESS…UTTER stillness had replaced the thundering of the avalanche, leaving a scene in its wake so serene it might have been beautiful had Altoneir not known what had stood on the side of the mountain mere minutes before. After taking a moment to orient himself, from examining the tree that had stopped his descent to using the shape of the mountain to determine which way Shaamel lay, he determined he had been taken almost half a mile from the lower outskirts of the settlement.

How was it possible that this still, snowy scene, interrupted only by the occasional glimpse of rooftop or debris, had been a thriving settlement in the arms of early spring? The very extremity of the change took Altoneir's breath away. Gathering himself, he began walking atop the glittering white, his pace increasing as he realized that, for the most part, the surface wouldn't yield under his footsteps. His movements, stilted with pain though he felt certain none of his bones had broken, exhibited none of his usual grace.

Thoughts of Aenwyn plagued him as he moved, his direction sure after centuries of life on that mountainside. The cold seeped through his brown leather shoes, but he barely noticed. Aenwyn…he had to find his mate.

No movement revealed any other survivors as he approached what was left of the settlement, realizing as it came into view that the serenity he had seen had been an illusion brought on by distance. Everywhere he looked, the blanket of snow was broken by pieces of the buildings it had destroyed and by the trunks of trees it had felled. Altoneir realized with horror about halfway to where his roundhouse had stood, the bodies of some of the elves of Shaamel had also been thrown amongst the debris.

Valeth's was the first body he found and, despite his frantic desire to find Aenwyn, Altoneir stopped for the quickest of moments to make sure the elf didn't need his help. One glimpse of the broken body and staring, bloodshot eyes before him told him Valeth was beyond aid, and he continued his trek upwards, quickening to a run as the reality of the situation crashed upon him. He had shielded Valeth and his shop, and yet…

When he reached the place where the roundhouse he had shared with his mate should have been, his heart splintered at what he saw: a simple expanse of white, so deep no sign of debris broke the surface at all.

"Aenwyn!" he shouted. If she had shielded, if his magic had been enough to protect her, perhaps she would hear him and make some sound to help him locate her.

There was no answer.

Altoneir stabbed at the area with his magic, feeling for any signs of the life he knew as well as his own. He wanted to scent her, to feel her life force, to know that even if she was injured, she had survived.

He felt nothing.

With a bellow of fear and anticipatory grief, Altoneir dropped to his knees and slammed his fists on the hard surface of the snow. Magic spread from every direction under his hands, and the ground broke in great fissures, spiderwebbing through the empty area and revealing what lay beneath.

He saw the roundhouse first, or what was left of it. The walls had collapsed along with the roof, and Altoneir glimpsed hints of their lives together as he searched for Aenwyn: the blue water-cloth coverlet from their bed, which Aenwyn herself had stitched and embroidered with enormous care. The small statue of a mountain wolf, carved from stone but set with two small emeralds for eyes, had broken into two pieces.

And then he saw the first sign of his mate: a pale hand seeming to reach for him from under the snow. Rushing to it, Altoneir took it in his own. Surrounded by the icy waste, he had prepared himself to feel the cold of death upon it; instead, its slight warmth, a warmth he refused to consider might yet be leaving her, gave him the first genuine hope he had felt since emerging.

The magic this time was less destructive than his initial cast; instead of forcing large fissures into the ground, Altoneir quickly but carefully carved the snow covering his mate's face into pieces, using cushions of air to move them out of the way.

It only took one glimpse for Altoneir to understand utterly and completely that Aenwyn, despite his protective spells, despite his order to her to shield herself, had not survived the disaster. The first thing Altoneir saw as her body was uncovered, the first thing he had sought as her body had come into view, were her beautiful, clear, blue eyes. Open and staring, Altoneir could see immediately that the life had left them, that the force and soul had left them. He didn't have to wonder why she hadn't closed them in death, for the undersides of her eyelids were packed with the same icy snow as...as her mouth and, Altoneir knew, her airways.

Once he allowed himself to gaze at the rest of her face, at the mouth wide open in a silent scream of protest against unwilling death, he knew the image would haunt him for the rest of his days. That scream, the silent scream she seemed to be forming even at this moment, could never have escaped, for her mouth was packed with rock-hard snow and ice.

Though somewhere inside of himself he knew he could not save her, Altoneir immediately went to work clearing the hateful obstruction. Without hesitation, he used the same gentle streams of heat he had used to shape the setting of her diamond not even an hour before to break the surface and begin melting the snow in her mouth. Once it had broken somewhat, Altoneir, as gently and lovingly as he had ever touched her, used one long finger to sweep the rest of it out of her until everything was clear.

As he had suspected, the snow had forced itself not only into her mouth, but down her throat, cutting off any chance she had to breathe, even if her nose hadn't been obstructed in the same way. Once it had been cleared, he gently pushed her chin upwards, closing off the silent scream and restoring her face to the pale oval he had loved for so long, her light freckles standing out against her chin just as they had in life. Half a thought toward the snow holding her eyelids aloft had him able to close her eyes as well, and then she might have been sleeping even if most of her body was still buried in snow. She might have been sleeping, with the golden red of her hair, encrusted with slush but still somehow beautiful, spread about her.

No tears pricked Altoneir's eyes as he worked to free the rest of her body from the snow and gathered her into his arms. His grief, immediate and life-shattering, went too deep for tears. Where she had been, vibrant and content and serene, only a gaping chasm remained, and he didn't know in that moment whether he could survive the rending of his world her loss had incurred.

He would never be certain how long he knelt in that hateful snow and held her body, perfect and whole in death, to his chest. It might have been minutes, but it might have been hours. Darkness had almost completely fallen by the time he lovingly laid her back on the ground and covered her in the green cloak he had worn that day.

"Forgive me," he whispered. "Forgive me, my love…my heart…my life."

His heart, which he had thought already shattered beyond repair, broke anew as he stood and gazed down at her before turning away and continuing into the settlement to look for other survivors, to look for his parents and hers, and to piece together anything that might have been left behind in the destruction's wake.

AYDUIN AND NALAEA, unlike Valeth and Aenwyn, bore no outward signs of trauma from the onslaught of the avalanche after Altoneir had unearthed them in much the same manner as he had his mate. Their bodies unbroken, their mouths unobstructed, and their eyes peacefully closed, they lay in the snow as though they had purposefully positioned themselves in death with their arms around each other, Nalaea's head resting on Ayduin's broad shoulder.

What did my mother do, Altoneir wondered, *to ensure they died peacefully?* More powerfully magical than her mate, it had to have been Nalaea who had kept the wake of the avalanche from destroying their bodies. But if she had done that, why had she not been able to save herself and his father?

Altoneir shook his head as he fought the mental images trying to infiltrate his mind. He did not want to imagine their deaths; he did not want to see the end of his parents' ancient lives for the rest of his days as he would the end of Aenwyn's. If he must have a memory of his parents' demise, he wanted it to be simply what he saw before him: two mates, peacefully entwined with one another, serene against the chaos surrounding them.

As he gazed at his parents while still seeing Aenwyn's silent scream in his mind's eye, Altoneir's grief took physical form at last. Crumpling to the cold ground, the strength in his body gone, Altoneir screamed out his pain to the empty skies before the sobs wracked his body and left him blind to everything around him, unaware of anything but his own immeasurable well of grief. Somewhere, through the sobs and screams, he had it in him to wonder if he was truly alone, if he was the only elf who had survived the destruction of Shaamel.

Even as the sobs spent themselves, Altoneir was unaware of the voices calling for him until a hand dropped heavily onto his shoulder. Though the touch was unexpected, Altoneir didn't flinch; he had no emotion left to even be surprised to have been found by others. Dully, he turned to look at the hand and then into the face of its owner: Paeral, the elf he had exchanged verbal blows with only that morning.

"Come," Paeral said softly, no trace of the snide enmity they usually shared. "You cannot help them."

Altoneir shook his head, though he wasn't entirely aware what he was denying. He knew his parents were gone, knew Aenwyn was gone, knew he couldn't help them, and yet...and yet, how could he possibly be expected to stand at Paeral's soft command? To stand, to talk to Paeral and the others Altoneir now saw standing behind him through his pain-blurred eyes, to move his body...it signaled both an end and a beginning he was not certain he would ever be ready to face.

Altoneir turned back to his parents, cold on the ground in their eternal embrace. He had used his cloak to cover Aenwyn — what was he to use to cover them? He couldn't leave them as they were, exposed to the world and its cruel elements.

"Altoneir."

The voice was not Paeral's, but a softer voice, female. She spoke his name like a soothing caress, no hint of the soft command Paeral had employed, but in a tone of sympathy and coaxing.

"Inaadi," Altoneir finally responded dully, not turning to look at Paeral's mate. His voice cracked on the word, the result of the screams and sobs of grief he had expressed only a few minutes before. He continued to stare at his parents' bodies as though he were entranced.

"Call your magic to cover them," Inaadi coaxed, somehow knowing what he sought, the act he had to complete before he could consider standing and taking that first step.

At her suggestion, Altoneir straightened. Their coverlet, the one of red and pink woven wool, had to be under the snow somewhere close to where his parents lay. He held out his hand toward his parents, palm down, and called it from wherever it had been before.

The coverlet appeared as though from thin air, hovering above them with no trace of snow, damage, or debris marring its bright colors. He had not called those things to him, so they had not come. Without moving his hand or his body, Altoneir guided the coverlet over his parents, covering them entirely until all that could be seen of them was the shape of their entwined bodies under the fabric.

"You have served them well," Inaadi said when he had lowered his hand, the small bit of magic somehow consuming the last of his power. "Join us."

The act of standing, the act of turning his back on his parents to face the small group of elves standing behind him, was almost more than Altoneir could stand. He whispered no words to his parents, made no final plea for absolution, as he tore his eyes away from the coverlet that contrasted so starkly with the white of the snow. As he stood and turned to face whomever was behind him, his movements were stilted with the immense pain of his injuries and the sorrow he now bore.

Six elves stood gathered, facing him as he turned, their faces as stark with grief as his own. Paeral and Inaadi stood close together, though not touching, watching him closely. Standing in a tight group next to them were Erlen, Rovyre, and Danala, a small family unit. Erlen grasped her daughter's hand, Rovyre standing protectively over both of them.

How did their whole family survive?

The only other elf who seemed as alone as Altoneir felt was Beimenor, who stood apart, the lines of grief starker in his face than in the others'. Altoneir realized that for him to be standing alone meant his mate had also not survived the disaster. Like Altoneir, Beimenor stood without a cloak, and Altoneir knew somehow that the cloak covered the body of Heilen somewhere else in the ruins.

"Are we the only ones left?" The question left his lips without warning, without thought, as he faced the others.

Paeral was the one who responded, looking at Altoneir with a stoicism uncharacteristic of him. "I believe so," he answered. "We have found no others, but we must begin the search at once."

The words, spoken in a matter-of-fact tone that belied the utter desolation all of them felt in that moment, were true. The first thing they had to do was search for more survivors and render aid if it was needed. After that…none of them wanted to think of what came after that.

Altoneir nodded at Paeral, a short, curt movement that showed his readiness to act, but also to allow Paeral to take leadership of their small group for the time being.

"We must split and search the settlement," Paeral said decisively, looking at each of them in turn. "None of us must venture alone. Inaadi and I will take the northernmost part." He did not mention that his own parents and Inaadi's lived in that section of the settlement, but they all took their cues from him and selected areas in which they might find their own families or friends.

After Erlen, Rovyre, and Danala had claimed the southern edges for their search, Altoneir looked at Beimenor, silently ceding their choice of search area to the other elf. Altoneir had no one left; perhaps Beimenor would be more fortunate.

Beimenor spoke at last, his deep voice laced with sadness. "We will take the middle, beginning with the eastern edges and working west."

"It is done," Paeral declared. "We will meet at the circle when we have completed our work."

Altoneir was the first to cast an elven light over his own head; the deepening darkness would render searching impossible without it. The others followed suit, bathing the area where Altoneir's parents' roundhouse had once stood in amber light. Paeral and Inaadi were the first to leave, entwining their hands as they headed north. Erlen, Rovyre, and Danala went next, murmuring amongst themselves as they went south.

Beimenor and Altoneir looked at one another. "Who do you seek?" Altoneir asked. The question was without inflection.

"The shopkeepers," Beimenor answered. "Most did not leave their shops when the avalanche came, and I would not have them be separated from their families." He did not need to add that he meant not only to reunite the living if there were any others, but to gather the bodies of families that they might be sent into the void together.

Altoneir spoke no words of either agreement or contest, and the two set off together to seek those who had faced the onslaught alone.

THOUGH ALL SEVEN of the surviving elves of Shaamel searched both magically and physically, by the time the moon had reached its zenith, they had found no others who had survived the avalanche. Most had been buried under the snow, many dying the way Aenwyn had, suffocated by snow in their mouths and airways. Altoneir, his shoulders hunching more with each discovery, knew each of those faces would be catalogued in his mind for the rest of his existence; he knew he would never forget how they had looked just like his mate.

Some of the other bodies had been broken in much the same way

Valeth's had been, bludgeoned by the debris of falling buildings and tossed about with the rapid movement of the wall of snow.

Despite what Beimenor had suggested, none of them had moved any of the bodies, nor burned them to send them properly into the void. They knew they would have to before the next day had ended lest the bodies be consumed by the carrion eaters, but for the moment they let the spell Altoneir had cast to prevent such an occurrence stand.

"We must rest," Erlen declared, and Altoneir thought those might have been the first words the female had spoken since they had gathered before their search. "Our bodies will give way if we do not tend to ourselves, and we cannot complete the work that must be done."

The others looked around; the path of destruction had been wide enough to cover Shaamel and then some, but they knew there was bare land to be found not a mile outside the borders of the settlement.

Inaadi added, "I have recovered some food stores from my family's home. They will be enough to sustain us for the night and into the morrow, but then we must find food elsewhere."

The others shifted where they stood. Though what Inaadi had done was undoubtedly necessary, the idea of pillaging supplies from the homes and buildings of their wrecked settlement was not one any of them found palatable.

"Thank you, Inaadi," Rovyre finally said. It was him, not Paeral, who led them to the western outskirts of Shaamel, all of them trekking through the glittering snow with their magical lights still flaring until they reached the edge of the avalanche's path.

"We will stop here," Paeral decreed. The ground was bereft of most snow, though some patches remained in areas the trees had kept shadowed during the early spring days.

Without a word, Altoneir conjured blankets for each of the elves, pulling them from the wardrobes of his home and his parents', just as Inaadi had done with the food. The bright colors of the blankets, mostly woven of warm, thick wool, brought a lump to his throat, for he remembered each one.

Paeral added to their supplies by conjuring thick furs from his own stores, having a greater supply of them than most because of Inaadi's profession as a hunter. Altoneir remembered, with his first flicker of distaste toward Paeral since the disaster, that the elf had always preferred rich accoutrements. He shook off the feeling; they would all be grateful for the comfort and warmth of the furs as they made camp on the cold ground.

All seven of them ceased to speak as they settled themselves, Erlen and Danala gathering wood for a larger-than-usual fire and the others spreading the blankets and furs as near to it as was safe. The flames flickered merrily, sending their warmth into the group as though it knew they needed it not only for physical comfort, but for emotional comfort as well. Sitting around the fire, they silently ate of the foodstuffs Inaadi had distributed. The food may as well have been of ash for all the taste they noticed; for tonight, eating was simply a vehicle to sustain themselves, but not something to enjoy.

When they had all settled onto their blankets, but before they had laid down to attempt to sleep, Paeral finally spoke. "We must decide what we shall do when our work here has been completed."

They all knew what that work was, but none of them offered any comment as he continued. "I would suggest we gather what supplies we can and make for Caalenor."

The declaration surprised no one. Caalenor, the great elven capital city, lay in their very mountain range, resting high in the Chilpar Mountains. There, they would reunite with friends and family, but also be able to find a place within the large city to begin their lives anew.

Altoneir thought of the other jewelcrafters in Caalenor, four males and two females, one of whom had taught him the craft before the Crossing. Yes, in Caalenor, he might find friends again. In Caalenor, he might bring the news of Shaamel's demise that others would know and honor the tragedy. In Caalenor, he might find Aenwyn's uncle and aunt, that he might mourn her death with them.

Altoneir nodded as the others, except for Beimenor, agreed readily that Caalenor would be their best destination, for none of them wished to stay in Shaamel past sending the people they had lost into the void with honor.

"It would be best to travel to Y'Nalone," Beimenor argued. "Caalenor sits nearly at the peak of their mountain and faces none of the danger that has befallen us here. Y'Nalone must be warned that they might prepare against this eventuality." His face stark with the same grief Altoneir knew must show upon his own, his plea was more impassioned than was the general habit of the calm and peaceful elves.

"We have lived in Shaamel for six hundred years," Rovyre responded, his voice slow and halting as he gave voice to that which they had avoided discussing. "Never before has the mountain threatened us so. It is my view that Y'Nalone is in no greater danger than any other mountain settlement, and their slope is not nearly so steep as ours."

Beimenor scowled. "We thought we lived in safety as well. It is incumbent upon us to spread the news of this danger to others. With proper fortifications and spellcasting, this may not have befallen us at all, and Heilen-" He broke off, his voice catching with pain even as his brown eyes lined with silver.

They sat silently for a time, each remembering the horror of the great wave of snow descending the slope and decimating their homes. It was hard to argue against warning others after what they had experienced; still, Rovyre had a point. What had happened to them could not have been predicted and, despite Beimenor's assertions, was unlikely to have been guarded against even with warning.

It was Paeral who broke the painful silence. "Though your heart speaks truly, Beimenor, the settlement of Y'Nalone has no need for our skills or occupations. After warning them, we would still be pressed to relocate to Caalenor, where we might be useful. Perhaps the solution is to go to Caalenor but to dispatch messages with all haste to other mountain settlements in the Chilpar Mountains and in the other ranges. Elvendom must not be as unprepared as we were."

Beimenor looked somewhat sour, and Altoneir wondered if he had another reason for wishing to venture to Y'Nalone. He decided to offer a small measure of hope. "After I have ventured to Caalenor and mourned my Aenwyn with what remains of her family, I will travel with you to Y'Nalone," he said, feeling a sense of satisfaction as Beimenor's face softened.

"It is settled, then," Danala said with finality. Barely having reached her first century of age, Altoneir was surprised to hear her speak in the presence of those so much older than she, especially when major decisions were being made. Though the elves had no official hierarchy of age, it was generally expected that the younger generations defer to the elders in such situations.

Paeral looked slightly dissatisfied, though what she had said agreed with his position. Altoneir knew his ofttimes rival felt the same way as he did about Danala being the decisive voice in this matter. Both elves, however, stayed silent. It would not do to sow dissent among their small number so soon after the tragedy.

Though none of them spoke about their task the following day, it was close to all of their minds as they lay on their blankets and wrapped themselves in Paeral's furs.

Though Paeral, Inaadi, and Rovyre's small family seemed to be sensitive to the lonely positions of Beimenor and Altoneir, Altoneir could not help but listen to the sounds of them settling down together, the blankets of the mates joined and Danala's not far from her parents'. The slight murmurings as they positioned themselves and pulled the blankets and furs tight and the swish of clothing and skin rubbing against one another were all obvious to the enhanced hearing of the elves.

Altoneir finally allowed his mind to drift back to his mate as he closed his eyes. Had it only been that afternoon that they had made their last attempt to make a child together? Had it only been that afternoon when she had gazed at him in wonder as he moved inside of her, both of them hoping and dreaming fervently of their future? Had it only been that evening when she had reached for him…

Altoneir opened his eyes before the image of Aenwyn reaching for him as the avalanche that would claim her life separated them. He didn't think he could bear seeing it again, even in his mind's eye, but he soon remembered that mental images were not formed only when one's eyes were closed as he relived the moment.

Though Altoneir's sobs had been spent, tears ran freely down his face and into his blankets as he saw her again, her image obscuring that of the dark forest around him, the fire, and his new companions. She reached for him, her face set in the soft smile he had loved so much, but as the wall of snow approached, her face contorted and she opened her mouth wide…revealing a mouthful of snow.

Altoneir did not sleep that night, and from the muffled sounds he continued to hear throughout their campsite, he did not think the others did, either.

LEAVING

The ashes of the dead darkened what was left of the village
of Shaamel as surely as if they had draped a burial shroud
over the entirety of their former home. Throughout the day following
the devastation of the avalanche, Altoneir, Paeral, and the rest worked
in tandem - not together, for there was too much to cover to do so,
but with a kind of separated camaraderie in which they could feel the
presence of the others across the settlement.

The burning of the dead had never been performative, even in the
times at which they might have had the luxury to make it so. As the
elves had known for centuries, to die was to leave this world and
simply become part of the void, the vast expanse of nothing
surrounding the world of the living. No spirits lived on; no ancestors
guided the actions of their descendants. To die was to finally and truly
leave the world and life behind. Thus, when an elf died, the burning of
their earthly bodies did not have a place in the grieving process; it was
simply something that must be done, an empty vessel that must be
destroyed.

Altoneir had been part of many burnings in his existence and had
even ignited the magical flames at many of them. He was never much
affected; even when the dead had been his own grandparents before

"

the Crossing, afflicted with the mysterious disease that had made its way through the elven population, the burning had been entirely separate from his grief, for grief belonged to the loss of companionship and love, not to the loss of a body.

The burning of the dead in Shaamel, however, was different. Altoneir realized as he burned the third body he had found in the brief hour since awakening that the sheer volume of the burnings today held its own weight, and such grief as they all felt could not be completely divorced from the process. Every body burned served as a reminder of another piece of the enormous loss, the loss not only of companionship and love, but the loss of an entire way of life.

Altoneir worked all day, using his magic and the work of his bruised, aching body to unearth the bodies from the now-melting snow before sending a spark of the consuming death-flame to erase their bodies from the earth. Each one felt like a blow; each familiar face sent into nothingness served as a reminder of the violent ending of so many lives only the day before.

He saved Aenwyn for last. Only after he had ignited the bodies of his parents did he traverse the distance to his own destroyed home. He had only looked upon them for a few moments, lifting the blanket covering them to see their faces one more time before they left him forever, before he had cast the flame.

As he walked, his face stoic even as his halting gait revealed the physical and emotional pain he continued to endure, he wanted to block out what he saw before him; wanted to but could not. Gone was the unbroken sheen of hard-packed snow over the settlement; gone was the stillness that had stunned him the day before. Even with only seven of the elves of Shaamel remaining, their recovery efforts had changed the landscape once again: now a veritable disaster zone of broken ground, debris, and bodies to be burned, nothing of what Shaamel had once been remained.

The ashes of the dead were heavy in the air when he reached Aenwyn. Altoneir gazed down at her body, its familiar shape still covered with the green cloak he had worn the day before. He didn't know if he could bear to lift it and gaze at her; he didn't know if the pain of that moment would fracture what was left of his soul.

He lifted his hand to perform the burning but found that he couldn't cast the spell. Not without seeing her again, not without kissing her one last time. Stumbling slightly for the first time that day, Altoneir knelt at her side and gingerly lifted the covering to reveal her face.

Though pale with tinges of blue brought on by her icy death, her face was still the most beautiful thing Altoneir had ever seen, and seeing it in calm repose was a balm of sorts after the horror of discovering her body the day before. Perhaps when he remembered her in death, he could now see her like this, calm and still, rather than silently screaming.

Though he knew it was nothing more than an affectation to kiss the body that was no longer hers, Altoneir didn't deny himself the impulse. He leaned down and pressed his lips against her forehead, closing his eyes and trying to replace the frigidity of her skin on his lips with his memories of her warmth and softness.

He drew away and stood, knowing this, his final burning, would be the most difficult. His hand shook as he extended it toward her body, her face still uncovered, and he willed the flame to consume her.

The death-flame took less than a minute to do its work, no more and no less than it had taken with the other bodies that day. That seemed somehow wrong to him; somewhere, in his well of immeasurable grief, he had expected this burning to somehow be different.

When her body had gone, its ashes floating on the slight breeze, Altoneir forced himself to turn his attention to what was left of their home, still mostly buried in the snow. He knew, as did the others, that he would need to take what supplies he could from it, but he also knew there were a few possessions he wanted, a few pieces of their life together. He didn't care if they would make his pack bulkier or heavier. He couldn't leave Shaamel with nothing more than his memory, with nothing left to touch.

The work was quick. Altoneir knew where to look for what he needed and wanted. He took blankets and some preserved food left from the winter, another cloak and some of his clothing, and the pack he kept for his rare hunts. The pack would need some repair, but he deemed it salvageable and set it aside with the rest while he searched for the items that might have been less necessary for his body but were more necessary for his heart.

First, he took the jeweled snood he had made her for their mating ceremony nearly a thousand years ago. Kept bright and shining with care, she had worn it often, and he had always thought the gleam of the silver and small flecks of diamond and lapis lazuli beautiful against the golden red of her hair. He took it and folded it inside one of the blankets, unwilling to risk damaging it as they traveled.

After that most prized possession was secured, the others did not hold nearly the significance, but still he delved, searching for any scrap of memory he could carry. Two empty crystal bottles, waiting to be filled with her healing potions, their corks secured tightly but not sealed with wax, came next. Finally, he took her gold-tipped pen…the pen she had used to write the verses no one but him was ever privileged to see.

Altoneir gathered the belongings he had taken from the wreckage, but he didn't immediately return to the makeshift camp as had been agreed that morning. Instead, he followed the familiar path to his shop for one last thing he wanted to take with him.

When he had unearthed the dwarven diamond and the setting he had been working over and tucked them into his bundle along with his smallest toolkit, he finally trudged to the clearing where they would spend one final night before the next morning's final departure from their settlement.

"You were foolish to expend all your magic," Rovyre was saying to his daughter as Altoneir entered the camp, trying to clear the smell of the burning bodies from his nose and mind.

"*Apa*, what choice did I have?" Danala protested. "We number only seven, and all were needed to attend to today's task." As they all had, she avoided naming exactly what they had done.

"You will have naught left to protect yourself," Erlen snapped, her voice sharper and more strained than was usual. "Your magic has not yet fully developed and yet you still spent it. Had you but mentioned your weariness, your father and I - "

"I am not a child," Danala said hotly. "You would do well to remember - "

What she wanted her mother to remember, however, was lost when Danala and the others saw Altoneir enter the camp carrying his belongings, and none of the members of the small family brought the issue up again.

"Altoneir," Inaadi greeted him, noting the belongings bundled in his arms, his empty pack slung over one shoulder.

Altoneir said nothing, merely nodding as he crossed to his own blankets and furs. Placing his belongings atop them, he sat and began to repair his pack.

On the other side of the fire, Paeral and Beimenor resumed an argument they had obviously begun before Altoneir had arrived.

"Going to Y'Nalone makes no sense," Paeral said, his voice showing the fraying of the unusual patience he had shown the day before. "We can warn others far more effectively via horseback messenger once we reach Caalenor. We would reach Y'Nalone only to - "

"I do not give a damn that you think there will not be occupations for us in Y'Nalone. They must be warned!" Beimenor's deep voice rose in volume as he pronounced each word, and the rest of them stopped what they were doing and looked at him.

He didn't look abashed at his loss of temper, but he did lower his voice as he continued, "If the same thing happens in Y'Nalone as did here, we - "

"The same thing will not happen," Paeral countered. "As we said yesterday, Beimenor, they are on a gentler slope than we are and are highly unlikely to be afflicted by the same occurrence. You are free to go your own way, but the rest of us travel to Caalenor on the morrow."

Beimenor cursed loudly and stood, stalking out of the camp on his long legs, his filthy blue robes swirling around him as though mirroring his agitation.

Altoneir turned his attention back to his pack as Inaadi touched her mate's shoulder softly. "Beimenor should not travel alone," she said, her voice gentle. "He has lost his mate and his friends."

Paeral shook her off. "Then Beimenor must travel with us. It is his choice and no one else's. Not one member of our party can be spared for his quest."

Inaadi said nothing more, and the camp lapsed into silence as everyone attended to their own needs. Beimenor didn't return until they were settled around the fire, eating the evening meal of venison from the deer Inaadi had hunted and killed for them in the early hours of the afternoon.

"I travel with you on the morrow," Beimenor said shortly as he entered the camp, offering no further explanation.

"I am glad to hear it," Inaadi said evenly when no other answer was forthcoming. "Come, sup with us. You must be famished."

"No," Beimenor said shortly. His deep voice seemed to resonate through the camp, and Altoneir wondered once again what the stakes in visiting Y'Nalone had been for Beimenor, what he had given up by agreeing to travel with them.

Beimenor went to his own blankets and, like the rest of them had, set about preparing his pack for the next day's departure.

"The weather should be fine for traveling," Erlen finally offered as they finished their meal. "The chill will invigorate us, and in the weeks of travel, it will only grow warmer."

Paeral grunted. "We would do better to hope for a lack of spring storms," he said, his voice querulous. "Caalenor lies so high on the mountain that it will barely be the end of winter there when we arrive. One snowstorm on our path could delay us for days, if not weeks, and we are not equipped to endure such conditions."

"We are well versed in survival on the mountain, my love," Inaadi pointed out. "Even if we do encounter a storm, we shall be able to endure it."

Inaadi's statement was met with a silence that spoke only too clearly of the elves' newfound fears of the mountain's conditions.

After the meal was over and the remains packed for their journey on the morrow, the sky was fully dark. Like the night before, they all retreated to their blankets and furs to rest. Altoneir again listened to the sounds of the mates and families settling down together, and again was struck by the loneliness that threatened the stability of his very soul.

He lay in his blankets, sleepless, for several hours. Unlike the night before, it seemed most of the others had actually gone to sleep, exhausted by the load of the work they had done that day. Altoneir could stand it no longer when he heard Inaadi murmuring in her sleep much as Aenwyn had often done, and he stood, trying to be quiet and considerate as he exited the camp, a new set of robes in his hand.

Altoneir made for the familiar stream that ran through the forest at the corner of Shaamel. The area he had once used was buried in snow, but he knew if he followed it downstream, he would find it clear. He only had to travel half a mile before he once again saw the water rushing over the rocks of its bed, and he stopped, kneeling before it.

He bathed his face; the water was cold and crisp, the result of snowmelt higher on the mountain, but he found it more refreshing than uncomfortable. With each splash of the water on his face, Altoneir banished the dark thoughts and images from his mind.

He removed his filthy clothing next; he had not changed since the avalanche had caught him the day before, and his robes were streaked with dirt and some small spots of blood from the scratches he had accumulated during his tumble through the snow. There was not enough light to see clearly, so after a moment, Altoneir conjured an elven light just above his head, bathing the small clearing in soft illumination.

Surveying his body for the first time, Altoneir noted the many bruises on his skin, the worst of which was a large purple and black splotch across the left side of his chest, extending onto his back. He knew that resulted from the tree he had tumbled into, the tree that had brought his descent to an abrupt stop. His other injuries were more minor, and he paid them no mind but to groan softly as his movement caused his right arm and leg to ache.

Chilled in the night air, he dressed himself quickly in the additional set of robes he had brought, sending a spark of magic towards himself to warm the fabric of the robes and his own skin. The water was cold enough; there was no reason the rest of him had to be uncomfortable as he did the chore he had set out to do.

Taking a small lump of perfumed soap from his bundle, Altoneir scrubbed out the spots and streaks on his brown robes from the day before. When he was satisfied, he submerged them in the stream to rinse them, relishing the cleansing feel of the cold water over his hands as he did so.

The task done, Altoneir directed his magic towards his sopping robes, now laid out on a rock beside the stream bed. With a rush of warm air that seemed to come from nowhere, the clothes dried quickly, leaving them almost as pristine as they had been when he had donned them the previous morning.

Altoneir gathered the now-clean robes into his arms along with what was left of the soap and headed back to the camp. He wasn't sure why, but somehow, he thought he might be able to sleep.

TURNING their backs on Shaamel was one of the hardest things any of the elves in the small traveling group had ever done. Even though Paeral had survived with his mate and Rovyre with his family, everyone left behind the memories of their former home and the loved ones who had perished in the avalanche, their ashes now dissipated and the evidence of their existence swept away as surely as they had entered the void. Shaamel had been their home for centuries, and the abrupt change in their circumstances, the destruction of all they had once known, was heavy on their hearts as they angled northwards toward Caalenor.

The traveling group split into four smaller bands almost immediately upon the commencement of their journey. Paeral and Inaadi, who began the journey hand-in-hand despite the heavy packs on their backs, led them into the forest. Rovyre, Erlen, and Danala clustered together a short distance behind, murmuring amongst themselves. Beimenor walked alone, his face hard, and Altoneir brought up the rear several feet behind the rest of them.

By silent agreement, all of them turned to gaze upon their home one last time before Shaamel disappeared behind the blossoming foliage of the mountain forest. Altoneir wasn't sure what any of them were expecting to see in that last look, but to him, it served as a reminder that their home no longer existed. From the short distance they had traveled, Shaamel was nothing more than a field of debris under melting snow with no real landmark left to mark it as the home they had all loved.

Nothing, Altoneir thought. *We leave nothing behind, nothing of who and what we once were.*

As he turned back to the trail with the others, the grief that had weighed heavily on him, the memories that had plagued him, faded into an emptiness so complete Altoneir thought his chest would cave in upon itself. As they began their long journey, none of them seemed to find the refined gait typical of elven travelers, as though they all had become something outside of themselves at that moment. With shoulders sagging and steps that marked the death knell of all they had known, they proceeded into the heart of the familiar forest as though their very grace had been diminished, as though they had become mortal, the land an enemy rather than a friend.

All the things Altoneir had once loved and cherished could not fill the emptiness that had overtaken. He knew, with a certain detached remembrance, that the forest was beautiful in the spring, the deciduous trees in full bloom of leaf and flower and the evergreens standing stately among them, a reminder that not everything faded in the winter. As he walked among the trees, the pace Paeral had set considerable but not demanding enough to tire them early in the day, Altoneir thought the beauty should have soothed something in his soul, but it could not reach him.

Altoneir said not a word as they camped the first night, then the second, then the third. No one seemed to notice his silence as they talked amongst themselves, usually forcing themselves to think ahead to Caalenor rather than behind to all they had lost in Shaamel. The conversations seemed so callous and shallow to his ears; how could they be planning for the future when Aenwyn was gone? When Ayduin and Nalaea's ancient lives had ended? When they had burned the broken bodies of their friends and family just days before?

His resentment built as they traversed a narrow valley between their mountain and the next, and he nurtured it as a balm to the emptiness he had felt upon leaving his home behind. He noticed to some satisfaction that Beimenor, though he occasionally contributed to the conversation, remained apart just as he did.

On the sixth evening of their journey, Paeral and Inaadi opted to share their evening meal apart from the others, some need driving them to be with one another, and one another only. That evening, Rovyre invited Beimenor and Altoneir to sit with his family and talk while they ate of the preserved fruit and meat they had scavenged from their settlement before they had left. Inaadi, though she had ventured away from them for a time to hunt for their meals, as she did almost every day, had come back empty-handed that day.

Altoneir only shook his head, having no wish to break his long silence nor to listen to them talk about Danala's prospects in Caalenor, the opportunity she would have to perfect her craft among the masters of the elven city, and their plans to build a roundhouse on the outskirts where they still might enjoy the quiet they had loved in Shaamel. He placed his belongings a small distance away from the rest of them, as he always did, and went about his evening rituals in the same silence that gave the only voice to the ruin of his soul.

To Altoneir's surprise, however, Beimenor joined Rovyre's family to sup that night, and, he noted, to talk. For the first time since they had left Shaamel, Beimenor did not confine his comments to simple agreement or disagreement but joined in the conversation about the trades- and craftsmen in Caalenor. It only took minutes before the elf was completely immersed, seeming to be a part of the group rather than one standing alone.

It made Altoneir sick to his stomach, and he tried to tune them out as he ate his small repast alone.

That night, Paeral and Inaadi remained apart from the group, though they had settled their blankets not far away, their own small fire crackling in a small clearing adjacent to the larger one they had chosen for their camp that night. Altoneir didn't much care, nor did he wonder why they had separated themselves from the group.

Altoneir had slept very little on the journey, his body only falling into true rest when it was so exhausted it could overtake the images in his mind's eye, the detached recollection of the tragedy that had befallen him. That night was like most of the others had been: listening to Rovyre's family murmur goodnights to one another and fall into sleep, listening to Beimenor toss and turn until he found his comfort among the forest detritus on the ground, and listening to Paeral and Inaadi snuggle into one another before falling asleep with their bodies entwined.

He could see the moon in the gap of the foliage above them, high above them and reaching its zenith. Only a small crescent tonight, it offered little light to the clearing, and even with his eyes wide open, only the small flickering of their fire allowed Altoneir to see the shapes of the elves around him. As the moon passed out of sight, he finally fell into an uneasy sleep.

THE NIGHTMARE WAS the same every night: the vision of the wall of snow coming for him, coming for Aenwyn; the vision of Aenwyn with her hand outstretched for him, her mouth wide and filled with snow, her eyes open in a hideous, dead gaze. As always, he jolted awake upon the onset of that final vision, the one that haunted him above all others, and as always, it took him a moment to orient himself and remember where he was and what had happened.

As his ragged breathing slowed, Altoneir became aware of sounds coming from Paeral and Inaadi's nearby camp that he had not heard yet on their journey: ragged breathing they were obviously trying to keep hushed, the tale-tell sound of skin against skin, the light moans as each of them found pleasure in the other's embrace.

As he listened, Altoneir realized why they had opted to camp apart from the others. In his rational mind, he knew he couldn't blame their desire to be close, to make love even. But in his empty heart he registered a rage so consuming he had to work not to roar out his fury into the night.

Mastering himself and trying to ignore the sounds coming from the adjacent camp, Altoneir gazed around him. The camp was familiar; though they were, by necessity, sleeping in a different place each night, the way they had set up the blankets, the size of the fire, the breathing of the elves round him, were all familiar. He tried to focus in on the sounds of the surrounding forest, tried to calm his own breathing, to rationalize out of himself the fight he so badly wanted to start for Paeral and Inaadi's casual disregard of his loneliness and pain.

His eyes caught on something he hadn't noticed before: Beimenor was not sleeping as far apart from the others as he had before. Instead of sleeping on the edge of the camp as he had been prone to do for the entire journey, he had moved his blankets into the small group of sleeping figures that marked Rovyre's family. Altoneir wondered if he had been invited to join them or whether he had simply decided he was weary of being apart.

Whatever the reason, though, Altoneir knew he couldn't take any more. He couldn't take watching Paeral and Inaadi travel together, loving one another through the pain of what they had been through and what they had lost. He couldn't take watching Beimenor slowly become part of Rovyre's family group while he himself could not bear the company of others. He no longer wanted to mourn Aenwyn with her uncle and aunt in Caalenor, and he no longer wanted to reform the ties he had once had to the jewelcrafters there.

He wanted to be alone, and he knew in that moment that he would welcome death as easily as he now welcomed solitude.

Altoneir stood as quietly as he could, not wanting to face the questions of the others, and began rolling his blankets and gathering what belongings he had removed from his pack. He left Paeral's fur behind; he wanted nothing with him that had belonged to anyone but himself or Aenwyn. Carefully, and not knowing why he did it, he used a fallen evergreen bough to sweep the evidence of his presence there completely away. Once he was done, only the carefully folded gray fur offered any sign that the area had been inhabited.

Satisfied that he had woken no one and knowing Paeral and Inaadi were still occupied with each other, Altoneir hefted his pack and left the camp, angling south for the wilds of the Chilpar Mountains.

BEASTS

Altoneir's enjoyment of his bath in the ice-cold stream somewhere in the northern Chilpar Mountains was short-lived. Though for a moment he had relished the bite of the frigid water as a balm to his dark thoughts and empty heart, he began shivering violently soon after immersing himself. Because even his magic was not sufficient to warm the entire stream, he did what he had always done when bathing in winter: he directed some heat at his body, rather than the surrounding water. A few seconds later, heat radiated from him, and his shivers subsided.

It was his first bath since leaving the other Shaamel elves. The intervening time had been spent following the game trails across the mountains, always keeping a southern bearing, and enduring the way they curved and doubled back on themselves sometimes in favor of following them rather than staying on the more established paths of his own kind. He was reasonably certain Paeral wouldn't have spared the time to look for him, but all the same, he didn't want to be found.

Sustenance had become a problem on the third day when his stores of preserved food had run out. Though Altoneir was a perfectly adept hunter, he was not as talented at tracking as Inaadi, who hunted as her profession. Not wanting to deviate too far from his trek southward, he had eaten from his pack until it was no longer an option.

As Altoneir emerged from the stream, clean and with a sopping bundle of robes in his arms, he thought of Aenwyn and, this time, of his parents as well. It seemed he could do nothing without it linking back to those he had lost, especially his mate. He lost his grip on his magic, and his body abruptly became cold again before he could pull on his other set of robes.

Had they been cold when they died, or had they suffocated before they could feel the freezing grip of the snow?

He knew there was no way Aenwyn could not have died cold; between the snow that had forced itself into her eyes, her mouth, and her nose, and the snow that had buried her, she must have been unbearably cold as she died. She must have felt the icy fingers of death physically as well as mentally as she struggled against the inevitable...

Altoneir gasped with the pain of the mental image. For the first time since they had left Shaamel, he was startled to feel hot tears on his cheek, chilling rapidly in the early spring air. The tears fell faster as he pulled on his robes and cloak, and by the time he was dressed again, they had increased until he was fully weeping.

He didn't dry the set of newly cleaned robes right away. Rather, he sat right on the ground by the stream and gave himself over to his sorrow. It was almost a relief after days of feeling the emptiness threaten to swallow him. Sadness and grief were better than *that*.

By the time Altoneir's tears ceased falling, he was so worn down he almost didn't take the time to venture from camp to search for food. Only by reminding himself that would die if he did not sustain himself did he manage to drop his belongings off at his small camp and venture forth into the surrounding forest.

The plants had not had time to fully develop since the end of winter, so Altoneir had no luck in finding anything edible that way. He did, however, spot a small rabbit separate from its warren. He felled it with a gentle brush of his magic, ensuring it didn't feel any pain or fear as it entered the void.

The scant bit of meat it provided sizzled over the small fire in his camp while he quickly burned the offal, trying not to focus on the memory of casting the death-flame over his parents and his mate. *The two are not the same*, he reminded himself.

The meat was not very flavorful because of his lack of salt or any other seasonings, but it didn't bother him overmuch as he ate it; this food was for sustenance, and enjoyment of it was secondary to that need. As he chewed the gamey meat, he wondered whether he would ever enjoy a meal in the company of others again. At that moment, wandering alone for the rest of his existence sounded more appealing than letting anyone else into his heart.

After he had eaten and stoked the fire, Altoneir went to his pack and retrieved the dwarven diamond and silver setting for the first time since leaving Shaamel. Casting a small elven light over himself, he once again considered the gemstone as he had before Aenwyn had died. The sparkling facets of it, just as bright as they had been before, seemed to mock him now.

He weighed the diamond in his hand, considering. If he were to finish crafting the setting and sell the piece to the landed nobles in the valley, he would have enough coin to survive for quite some time, perhaps until he was ready to enter society again, if he ever was. He knew he would have no trouble finding a buyer among them; he had sold to the minor nobles that ruled the small villages before, and this piece promised to be unique. After another minute of contemplation, Altoneir put the diamond and its unfinished setting back into his pack. He just couldn't stomach the idea of working on it yet - it had been meant for Aenwyn, and now she would never wear it. Though he knew he would eventually need to, he couldn't abide the idea of selling it to someone else.

Extinguishing the elven light and moving only by the light of the moon and his small fire, Altoneir settled into his blankets for the night. As he drifted off, he hoped, as he always did, that his sleep might be uninterrupted by the nightmares that had plagued him since the avalanche.

And as always, he woke panting in the night, the mental image of his dead loved ones fresh in his mind.

~

ALTONEIR, by necessity, had to traverse the known trails the next day, for the winding game trail he had been following had veered higher in elevation than he wanted to travel. Despite that, he was surprised when he heard the footsteps of the travelers around a bend, and he had a moment to decide whether to stay out of sight or greet them. After so many days of traveling alone, he decided to show himself, secure in the knowledge that the group was not Paeral and the others come to look for him.

He didn't make a grand entrance or even speak at first; he simply stopped and waited along the side of the trail for the travelers to come into view. When they saw him, they halted as well, their faces looking surprised to see someone so far from the settlements, but not shocked or displeased. Altoneir knew he did not look as he felt; he had bathed the night before and was wearing a clean set of robes. They would not have been able to tell by looking at him how long he had been traveling alone.

"Greetings," one of them, a tall, sandy-haired male, said. "I am Daenan, and my companions are Biris and my mate Ularen. We travel to Caalenor from our home in the Gray Hills." His voice, steady and even, was welcoming in the way that elves always welcomed others of their kind, with peace, goodwill, and good intention.

Altoneir inclined his head, willing himself to find his voice, to find the comfort he had once felt around other elves. "Altoneir," he said finally, his voice raspy from disuse.

The three elves waited for more information, but when none was forthcoming, the female, Ularen, spread her hands in a gesture of welcome. "We were about to stop for our midday meal," she said. "Would you not join us, Altoneir?"

Altoneir considered, and his hesitation seemed to surprise them. They glanced at each other, clearly discomfited by this solitary stranger in the forests of the Chilpar Mountains. Elves were not solitary creatures by nature; they thrived on peaceful communion with one another, whether through long acquaintance or new meeting. To find him alone was surprising enough; his hesitancy to join them in a meal was nearly shocking.

Making up his mind, Altoneir inclined his head again. "It would be my honor," he told them. "It has been many days since I have seen others of our kind." He didn't tell them, of course, that it had been Daenan's declaration of his bond with Ularen that had made him hesitate.

All three smiled at his acceptance, some of their doubts already calmed as Altoneir answered in the way almost any other elf would have. They surprised him, however, by not proceeding into a forest clearing, but taking their packs off their backs right on the side of the trail. Ularen rummaged through hers until she pulled out several bundles of various sizes. Altoneir took out his waterskin, his wineskin having long since been depleted, and what was left of the meat he had cooked the night before.

Daenan eyed Altoneir's spread but chose not to comment on the scantness of it. Instead, he held out a packet of dried berries, a kind offer to one who had tasted nothing but meat and water for days. Altoneir accepted the packet with a small smile of thanks, the first smile he had worn since Aenwyn's death. "My thanks," he said. "I travel toward the valley and the settlement my people abandoned."

He surprised himself with the declaration, for he had not put his destination into words even to himself until that point. Though he couldn't articulate why he wanted to travel to his former settlement of Y'Sathemar, which his people had abandoned for Shaamel when the humans had come to Ilbeor and the treaty had been signed, he felt an inexplicable pull toward the first home he had shared with Aenwyn.

Biris spoke for the first time. "Why do you seek settlement in the valley?" he asked after he had swallowed his meat. "The humans have inhabited it for centuries. You won't find many of our kind there." Indeed, after the ancient elves had signed the treaty with humans, opting to cede the valley in exchange for a lack of open war, most elves had not dwelt there.

"I am uncertain where I will seek settlement," Altoneir answered. "At this moment, I simply want to visit my former home."

The four elves were silent for a few moments, all of them lost in thought. Finally, it was Ularen who asked, "Why do you travel so far alone, Altoneir?" The question sounded tentative, but Altoneir knew it was a valid one. Traveling so far without companions was unusual among elvenkind.

He swallowed, knowing it was time to share the news of Shaamel for the first, but certainly not the last, time. "My settlement, Shaamel, has been destroyed. My mate and parents did not survive."

Though the words were plain, the emotion welling behind them threatened to crest and devour Altoneir whole.

The three elves looked shocked, as well they might. The decimation of an entire settlement was disquieting news. Daenan broke the momentary silence. "I am so very sorry," he said, his baritone voice dripping with compassion for the devastation he knew Altoneir must feel. "Will you tell us what happened? We have not heard of misfortune on such a scale in our entire lives."

"It was an avalanche," Altoneir began. "It came down from the slopes above Shaamel nearly three weeks ago. It destroyed everything in its path."

Ularen shifted in her place, clearly not certain she wanted to hear more than what he had already said. She didn't protest, however, when Biris encouraged Altoneir to go on.

The details Altoneir shared were the barest of sorts. He didn't describe the nightmares that plagued him about how Aenwyn had died, didn't describe the broken bodies of many of his friends. He simply told them how quickly it had all happened, how Shaamel had been essentially wiped off the face of the mountain, and how there had only been seven survivors, including himself.

Altoneir knew the next question was coming before Biris spoke it. "If there were seven survivors, why do you not travel with them? I would think you would enjoy the companionship of those from your settlement after everything you lost."

"I did not wish to travel to Caalenor," Altoneir said, offering no further explanation.

The three elves glanced at one another, and Altoneir thought he could almost read their thoughts. They had been about to offer to allow him to join their traveling party, but upon that declaration, they were at a loss for what to do, since their destination was the very one he did not wish to visit.

Altoneir spared them the effort of finding another offer to make him. "Traveling alone has allowed me to clear my thoughts," he said, making his voice gentler than it had been since the tragedy. "I will continue to the valley and perhaps after that will go to the dwarves in the Gray Hills before finding a new elven settlement. I am a jewel-crafter by trade and would see the jewels of the dwarves as I rebuild my supplies for my profession."

The tension between the three travelers eased significantly at Altoneir's declaration of his plan after visiting the valley, though he had fabricated it on the spot to offset further questions and offers. It could not have been clearer that they had been worried about his state of mind given such an unusual destination. The compassion and concern elves had cultivated within their culture since before the Crossing compelled them to help one who was suffering, as Altoneir clearly was, but hearing his end goal eased their minds.

Ularen began refastening the straps of her pack after putting away the wrappings from their midday meal. She hesitated, and then withdrew her hand, holding another packet of berries. "For your travels," she told Altoneir. "You will not find much plant life ready for harvest on your way down to the valley."

Altoneir accepted the packet with a nod of thanks.

"You are certain you cannot be convinced to travel with us?" Daenan asked, though the offer had never actually been made in so many words.

"I thank you for your kindness in including me," Altoneir said firmly. "But I prefer to remain alone while I mourn those I have lost."

"Of course," Biris murmured, and something in his voice caught Altoneir's attention. He wondered whether Biris had lost his mate or someone else dear to him, that he might understand Altoneir's grief in a way the other two could not. He couldn't find it within himself to be curious enough to ask.

Their packs retied, the three elves stood in unison, and Altoneir followed suit. "We wish you all the best, Altoneir," Daenan said, his voice somewhat more formal than it had been only moments before.

Altoneir inclined his head before hefting his pack and continuing south, angling down the mountain. Behind him, he heard the three travelers talking softly to one another as they continued their journey north to Caalenor.

THOUGH ALTONEIR HAD FOUND A DETACHED, short-lived sense of camaraderie with the three elves he had met on the trails, he was glad when he was on his own again. He hadn't anticipated how hard it would be to tell others what had happened in Shaamel, and he hadn't been prepared for the quizzical and sometimes pitying glances he had gotten from them as he had told his tale of loss. Though he understood why they had tried to convince him to come to Caalenor with him, he hadn't even had the slightest bit of temptation over the offer.

I'm better off on my own.

As he had somewhat impulsively told Daenan, Ularen, and Biris, Altoneir continued southwards but started cutting down the mountain as well, his aim the valley below and the abandoned settlement of Y'Sathemar. He had heard the humans in the valley had taken it for their own, but he still thought he might like to see it, might like to relive the early days of his mating with Aenwyn. It seemed as good a destination as any, and he could very well do what he had claimed and cross the valley to the Gray Hills, the dwarven smiths, and the elven settlements there.

Three days passed in which Altoneir couldn't find food for himself. Though he ventured further off the trails than he had before, though he used the skills he had learned over the centuries in his personal hunts, there was simply no game to be found. And as his state deteriorated, as hunger that could not be quenched by drinking copious amounts of water set in, Altoneir's grief again dulled into the abject, intolerable emptiness.

On the fourth day with no food, Altoneir stalked around the area he had chosen for his camp, looking for any sign of anything he could hunt for his dinner. He circled farther and farther out, examining the bushes for movement, looking for tracks and droppings, and listening for the slightest sound above the normal hum of life in the forest. He found nothing and, realizing he didn't have enough daylight left for a proper hunt, he headed back to his camp. Tomorrow, he would devote the entire day to the hunt; in fact, he would devote as many days as he needed to finding food for himself. Having never experienced hunger in his entire existence, he knew the feeling was not one he wanted to repeat.

On his way back to camp, Altoneir spotted a patch of mint leaves growing in a sunny patch on the forest floor. He stripped the entire patch, taking leaves by the handful and stuffing his pockets with them. Though he knew the mint would do little to stave off his hunger, it was the first edible thing he had found in days. He thought it might ease the ache in his belly and give some strength to his flagging limbs.

He chewed the first of the mint leaves as he walked, filling his mouth with the earthy, cooling flavor of them. By the time night had fallen, he had eaten all of them, and he felt little improvement in his physical state. As he lay down to sleep, his head swam and his stomach growled, putting a fine point on the misery that had been the past week.

A low snarl woke him from a deep sleep, and he sat up with preternatural quickness as he let his eyes adjust to the light. There - on the outer edges of his camp - stood an *allihr*, tall and proud but deformed-looking, as any wolf that stood on two feet might be. With matted gray fur and piercing yellow eyes, a pronounced snout, and a large black nose, the thing was almost entirely canine, but for how it traveled. *Allihr* never stood on all four paws.

Altoneir stood slowly, recognizing it for what it was. He had to be careful, for he knew *allihr* never hunted alone. If he was to protect himself from many foes, he had to know where they were. Instinctively, he shielded himself as he had the day of the avalanche, and the very feeling of it sent a jolt of panic and remembered fear through him.

The beast showed its fangs, almost seeming to smile in anticipation of the easy meal it saw before it. For a wild moment, Altoneir wondered if the *allihr* had been having as much trouble finding food as he had been, before realizing he didn't care. This beast, this thing of nature, wanted to end his life just as the avalanche had ended Aenwyn's. *Allihr* were a particularly vile form of predator in the eyes of most elves, for they killed not only for sustenance, but for sport. They were the only known animals who would leave an entire carcass behind if they were not hungry; they were the only known animals who killed for any reason other than their own survival.

It snarled again, and this time the sound was echoed by no fewer than six more of the beasts. From the sound of it, they surrounded his camp, even if they were too far from the ring of the dying firelight to be visible. Though he had felt a jolt of fear upon initially waking, Altoneir no longer felt anything of the sort. Instead, icy rage filled him, and he knew that the *allihr's* penchant for signaling one another with growls and snarls would be their downfall. His face hardened, all signs of fatigue replaced by a grim and furious determination as he widened his stance.

He reached for his magic, the sensation as familiar as anything else about his body and mind, and released his shield. Unlike he had done with the smaller game he had hunted in the forests, he did not kill the *allihr* mercifully. No, the *allihr* was after blood - *his* blood - and nothing about the fury he felt was kind.

He let his magic tear through him, holding out his hand toward the *allihr* and causing a fine blade of red light to erupt from it. The beast didn't have time to react before the magic removed its fanged head from its shoulders.

One of the *allihr* along the edge of the campsite howled, and whether it was a signal or a sign of distress for their fallen leader, Altoneir did not know or care. He whipped around, his robes billowing, and shot his magic toward the sound, ending it with an abruptness that was almost merciful.

Altoneir knew he wanted to rip into the rest of the pack, and he did just that. As they swarmed him, he let a lasting red light form between his hands, replenishing itself after each attack it made. The earlier fatigue he had felt from lack of food disappeared entirely as he allowed his deep well of magic to surge inside of him without restraint or thought, allowed it to give him energy even as it fueled itself.

Their deaths weren't quick. No, instead of decapitating them, Altoneir removed limbs, eviscerated their exposed underbellies, and used his magic to bludgeon them. His fury only grew as he attacked again and again, whirling about with such a swiftness that even the *allihr*, born apex predators, couldn't keep up with him. They never landed even one blow.

The four *allihr* surrounding him were not dead; no, they were lying in sticky pools of their own blood, panting and whining as the pain of their injuries overtook them. The last one standing seemed to take stock of the situation, with intelligence in its eyes Altoneir hadn't seen from the others. After the space of a single heartbeat, the beast turned and ran.

Altoneir wasn't sure whether he'd ever seen a predator run from a fight like that, but then, he had never fought the *allihr* before. It was rumored they had almost the cleverness of humans, if not the elves. Perhaps this one had realized it couldn't survive the confrontation.

Altoneir didn't even consider letting it go. Instead, he gave chase, the red light still glowing between his hands. With the enhanced speed of his kind, he caught up quickly and released his magic once again. A large slash appeared across the entirety of the beast's back, causing it to arch and roar in pain and fury before it stumbled and fell.

Altoneir stalked toward it, magic seeming to radiate off his entire being. Using the toe of his boot to heave it over onto its back, he growled, "I want to see the light leave your eyes."

The *allihr* apparently had no fight left; Altoneir's slash had severed muscles and tendons from its back, and it could not move as he stood over it. "Vermin like you shouldn't exist," Altoneir stated before decapitating it and finally releasing the brutal battle magic he had stoked with his rage.

He turned his back on it; there would be no dignified burning for these beasts. Let them rot for the carrion eaters.

As he strode toward his bloody camp, images of what he had done filled his mind, images of blood and bone and sinew, replacing his persistent vision of Aenwyn in death. He had killed all of them; no, he had butchered them. He had made them bleed and hurt; he had made them fear him.

And it felt good.

DESCENT

*A*ltoneir didn't move his fire or his campsite. As he skinned and cooked the first *allihr*, the one who had challenged him and woken him from his sleep, he sat amongst the blood and bodies of the other fallen members of its pack. The carnage didn't bother him; as a matter of fact, he found it to be a balm to his spirit, to know that he had power, that he could ensure his own survival amongst the ravages of a nature he was beginning to understand was cruel and unforgiving.

In the initial weeks after he had lost Aenwyn, his parents, and his friends, Altoneir had thought he wanted to die, too. He had thought that it would be better to simply cease to exist than to live with the pain of his loss. Though he did not believe he would see them again after death, he had thought there would be a certain symmetry in the end of all he had known, even of himself.

The encounter with the *allihr* and their subsequent destruction had taught him differently. He knew now he did not want his existence to be wiped out; he knew now that he still had something to live for even if he could not yet identify what that was. He had fought for his own survival, and he had won.

As the first of the *allihr* meat finished cooking over the spit he had fashioned, he noted the general lack of color. It had cooked to a dull gray with black spots from the searing of the fire, not to the appetizing brown and pink he was accustomed to from other meats. As he removed the piece of the *allihr's* breast from the fire, he thought ruefully of his lack of seasoning and salt. He had not thought to gather herbs for the cooking, and now he faced eating this gray meat without them or the delectable sauces Aenwyn had once made.

Altoneir did not use his knife to cut the meat. Instead, he simply held it in his hands, bringing it up to his mouth to tear a piece off with his teeth. Before, he would never have been so uncivilized; before, he had always been around others. Now, manners were no longer of any consequence.

The meat tasted as gray as it looked. Without seasoning, salt, or sauce, the taste was not even the gamey taste of venison or rabbit; it was a dull taste, a taste that suggested a meal more suited to being endured than enjoyed. The *allihr* had been so very lean; no fat marbled the piece he had cooked to add flavor and richness, and he doubted he would find much anywhere on the body. Still, however, Altoneir enjoyed the meal and finished the entire breast piece in his hunger, even gnawing the bones for their marrow when the meat was gone.

For the first time in days, Altoneir no longer felt hungry. In fact, he felt full and powerful again, as though the food had already returned the elven strength to his limbs and even to his mind. The fog of hunger was gone, as was the discomfort, and he felt no small satisfaction in knowing that he had brought it about by besting the beasts in what could only be described as a battle rather than a hunt.

When he was finished, Altoneir carefully sliced several more pieces from the skinned body of the allihr. One after another, he cooked them to the same gray and black finish of that first piece, then he wrapped them in the large leaves of the oak tree above his campsite and stowed them in his pack. He would not be hungry again while he traversed the trails down the mountain and into the valley; he would make sure of that.

The valley…as he listened to a piece of the *allihr's* leg muscle sizzle on the spit, he thought of his idea to go to the valley to visit Y'Sathemar, where he and Aenwyn had started their lives together. They had been happy there before the treaty had decreed they move into the mountains; they had lived a peaceful life among the swaying grasses, farming and raising animals, practicing their professions, and communing with their fellow elves.

Though they had experienced a few damaging storms over the centuries they had lived there, nothing had happened that in any way compared to the devastation wrought by the mountainside avalanche. The valley was safer...the valley was more fertile...the valley was more peaceful and temperate. When the humans had arrived, they had noticed those things, too. And they had insisted upon taking it for themselves, ceding the opportunity for the greater swaths of space the mountains offered in favor of confining themselves to the valley and allowing the elves and dwarves the mountains for their homes.

Altoneir had not been alone in his bitterness when their village had been ordered to be ceded to the humans; he had not been alone in wondering why the ancient ones of Caalenor had not fought to keep the lands they had inhabited since the Crossing. The elves could have won the ensuing war with ease; could have perhaps stopped the human race in its tracks. But those thoughts were anathema to the ancient elves, and counter to the purpose they lived by: to use their magic for help and healing rather than destruction. To coexist peacefully with other beings, just as they had with the fae on Aidawyra. It had been those predilections that had led to them ceding the smaller, if safer and more fertile, lands to the humans.

The treaty had been very clear: once the humans had taken possession of the valley, no elves were to dwell there but by express permission from the human royal family. Several centuries after it was created and signed by both races, one village of elves had been allowed to move back into the southern valley, but the reason behind their existence there was based not upon the elves' needs but upon a desire to help humans. Isasari was a settlement mostly composed of elven healers who the humans would call upon when their herbalists were not sufficient for their needs. Over the past two centuries since it had been built, Isasari had expanded to include all the occupations and diversity of a full elven settlement, but their primary purpose was still to provide healing services to the valley.

Altoneir had no desire to live the rest of his existence in the service of the humans who had taken their homes from them and exiled them to the mountains. He knew that when he came to the valley, he would not dwell in Isasari, but elsewhere, whether or not the humans gave him permission.

His anger grew as he considered the proposition, along with a single certainty that plagued him as he packed up the camp and prepared to descend the mountain: if the humans had never come or if they had not insisted upon taking the valley for themselves, Aenwyn would still be alive.

THOUGH ALTONEIR no longer eschewed the trails that led from the base of the Chilpar Mountains to the elven city of Caalenor, he saw no other elves as he descended toward the wide valley below. He had known Paeral would not take the time or spare the members of their party to look for him, but he found himself a strange combination of relieved and desolate as he spent day after day with no company but his own.

His thoughts festered; since he had come to the realization that the actions of the valley humans had led to Aenwyn's death, if only indirectly, his anger at their entire race persisted. At first, he tried to reason his way out of it. After all, humans were not long-lived like the elves. The humans who lived in the valley now and the humans who ruled from the lone mountain in the north were only distant descendants of the ones who had treated with the elves upon their arrival in Ilbeor. When he had sold the products of his profession to the minor nobles in the valley, they had seemed nothing but accommodating, even if they had a penchant for wanting to buy his goods for much less than their value.

Humans are not my enemies.

He kept forcing that thought into his mind, but it became increasingly difficult. Every time he dreamed of Aenwyn in death, every time the haunting picture showed itself in his mind's eye, his thoughts immediately homed in on the realization he had made as he had cooked the *allihr* so many days before: if they had still dwelled in Y'Sathemar, Aenwyn would still be alive. And the reason they had to leave their life there behind was the treaty with the humans, the humans in their greed and hubris, the humans...

Humans are not my enemies.

He repeated the mantra less and less as he neared the valley and the humans that inhabited it. No matter what he tried, the idea that the humans were ultimately responsible for the elves having been in Shaamel in the first place just wouldn't leave his mind. Sometimes, he could banish it with reasoned thought, but other times his rage grew until he felt almost as violent as he had when he had battled the *allihr*.

He estimated three more days of travel before he reached the valley, and he imagined he could smell the cook fires of the humans below him. Each waft of the nonexistent scent threatened to overwhelm him, though somewhere in his mind he recognized that the odor was a figment of his imagination.

They are alive. She is not. My parents are not. My community is not.

All at once, his rage overtook him and he lashed out with his magic before he knew what he was doing, sending a large evergreen crashing to the forest floor, its trunk ground in two as though it had been hit with a giant fist. He looked at the felled tree, willing himself to feel regret at the end of its ancient life, but he felt nothing but the fury that had overtaken him.

Abandoning reason and any attempt at calm, Altoneir began his trek down the trails again, striking out at the plant life all around him. He not only felled trees with the same bludgeoning magic he had used before, but he set brush afire before dousing it with water, and he threw stones off his path with blasts of air so strong they damaged whatever they hit. He knew anyone who came behind him would think a wild beast had passed through, perhaps enraged with disease or on the hunt. He didn't care in the least.

When he finally stopped, his breathing ragged and heavy, he bent over and placed his hands on his knees before vomiting all over the trail from exertion and distress.

Somehow, the vomiting bothered him more than the path of destruction he had wrought. As he stared at the gray chunks of half-digested *allihr* mixed with the yellow bile on the ground, he regretted his loss of physical control far more than he regretted his loss of mental and emotional control. He needed the food for strength, and he hadn't hunted again since he had killed the *allihr* and left what was left of their bodies behind.

It was high time to stop for the evening, and he had covered more ground than he had expected to in his wrathful destruction of everything around him. He walked farther, leaving both the destruction and the contents of his stomach behind, before he veered off the established trail into a small clearing, barely big enough for him to build a fire and spread his blankets.

As he lay on his bedding and picked at a fraying edge of the green woolen blanket, he did not try to calm himself. Instead, his mind on his dwindling supply of *allihr* meat, he thought about hunting before he reached the valley. He thought about finding wildlife in the forest as he had before, but he didn't think about killing it mercifully this time. No, he remembered all too clearly being drunk off the power that had stemmed from the *allihr's* fear, and he knew he wanted to feel that again…he knew, and he didn't even care that to do it he would have to cause suffering.

He wanted to feel alive again.

Altoneir took a deep breath as he crossed the edge of the forested mountains and took his first step into the valley. The air smelled sweeter here, of wildflowers and grass and soil, the temperature warmer than it had been on the mountain. In the valley, spring had truly arrived and though he knew the nights might still be cool, he welcomed the warmth of the sun on his face as he stared over the long, swaying grasses spreading in a sea before him.

His rage and search for feeling had lasted all the way down the mountain, and he had supped well in the past days on animals he had hunted with his wrathful battle magic. He didn't regret the kills; in fact, now that he stood on the edge of the expanse of grass, he was glad of the meals he had eaten and the cold, cooked meat residing in its leafy packaging in his pack. Though the valley would offer abundant wildlife and plants for him to consume, he knew he would have to be careful of causing a spectacle as he had in the forests; here, his wrath would be harder to conceal, and conceal it, he must.

He breathed in again through his nose, and he felt a calm wash over him unlike anything he had felt in weeks. He hadn't realized he would feel anything but fury upon reaching the human-inhabited part of Ilbeor, but instead he felt a sense of peace and safety. Here, the weather was more temperate. Here, no chances of rockfalls or avalanches threatened the inhabitants. Here, there were no steep climbs or descents, no boulders interrupting the landscape, and no concealed dangers. The valley was a place of tranquility, and instead of enraging him, it brought him comfort.

He knew from the changing light that the sun was already beginning to set behind the mountains at his back, and he decided to camp along the edge of the valley before setting off in the morning - where, he was no longer certain.

Altoneir hummed a slow, soothing melody his mother had often sung in Shaamel as she went about her work. The tune was not happy, had never been happy, and it was made more poignant by the grief that coursed through him as he remembered her, but like the valley itself, it gave him a sense of tranquility as he worked.

Clearing the grass in a large circle with a simple wave of his hand, Altoneir built his small cook fire even though he had little he needed to cook that night; some nettle tea to soothe his dusty throat sounded good, and he would enjoy the tiny licks of heat as he settled in. As it heated, he unrolled his blankets once again, sitting upon them in the dying light, his pack next to him and a small bundle he had not touched in some time in his hands.

He was tired of living off the land with the meager skills he had. He had never chosen to be a hunter, a farmer, or a gatherer; jewel-crafting had been his profession since he was only sixteen years of age, over two millennia ago and before the elves had made the Crossing to Ilbeor. Though he could survive, as most elves could, in the wilds, he knew he would never find that life fulfilling or fruitful. But to change that, to ply his craft again and to purchase the things he needed to survive, he had to address the one jewel he had taken from his shop in Shaamel before they had left the settlement behind.

Altoneir's pale, slender fingers shook slightly as he unwound the dwarven diamond and its setting from its blue fabric casing, and he prepared himself for the rush of longing he knew he would feel when it was revealed. As the multifaceted stone fell into his hands, clinking softly against the silver of its unfinished setting, he rode the wave of remembered hopes and allowed the grief of them to settle over him like a blanket.

This was meant for her.

He tried to banish the thought, tried to stymie the wave of remembered emotion as he had worked over it for her on that last day of life in Shaamel. He needed this stone, this setting, to forge a life for himself. Finished, the piece would fetch a price that would allow him to get what he needed to survive but also to buy some smaller, less opulent stones and the silver for settings from the dwarves in the Gray Hills to begin his work anew. He had chosen to bring the diamond with him for the memories he had of crafting it for Aenwyn, but now he knew he would need it to survive. He cursed himself for his lack of foresight in bringing other, lesser materials from his shop; at the time, he had only wanted that which reminded him of her.

Forcing his fingers to steady, Altoneir set the stone aside after turning it in his hands once more. He realized the light from his fire would no longer be enough for him to see the work in front of him, so he set a small, magical elven light just over his head.

He had brought the supplies he needed, though he hadn't considered them until just that moment. Talented though he was with his hands and with magic, he would still need the fine metal tools he had kept for centuries to ply his craft. He put the setting next to the diamond and rummaged through his pack for the lumpy bundle of instruments.

As he began to work, Altoneir stopped trying to stem the flow of memories and longing. With each change he made to the diamond's facets, he imagined Aenwyn's face catching the scattered light of its reflection. Though the image was a beautiful reprieve from those terrible visions that plagued him in the night, he did not stop the tears that blurred his vision as they flowed down his face, but waited for them to ebb before he set to work again.

As the night wore on, the tears eventually stopped, and Altoneir found himself working at a feverish pace rather than with the slow, meticulous care he usually took with his endeavors. His small instruments cut and shaped the diamond and setting in a blur of motion, his beams of heat piercing from his fingers like tiny rays of starlight. The work had not become a balm as he had hoped it would; it had become a fanatical obsession, and he knew he could not rest until it was done.

He was not certain how long he worked, only that the fire had diminished to embers and the moon passed it zenith before he stopped, the completed piece in his hand. The stone, cut so differently from any he had ever seen so that it seemed to glitter with its own light, sat proudly and securely in the setting he had created for it, a simple half-circlet wreathed by the tiny wildflowers Ayduin had wrought into the silver, wildflowers so detailed Altoneir almost thought they could have grown in the verdant valley itself. Affixed by both craft and magic, the glittering gemstone lent what almost seemed to be white sunlight to the beautiful setting, and Altoneir knew he had created something unique.

Threading it onto the fine silver chain he had brought for it, he held the necklace just below the elven light, allowing it to catch the beams that came down. It was truly beautiful, and for the first time since he had started working on it that night, Altoneir's thoughts were not on Aenwyn, but simply upon the beauty of what he had created. It soothed a jagged part of his soul, somehow.

Knowing the price it would fetch would be considerable, Altoneir briefly thought of eschewing the lower valley in favor of taking the piece to the Royal Mountain and the city of Emelle, where the high nobles and royalty lived. He knew he had created something those haughty humans would consider worthy of their stations, and he knew he would be paid handsomely by whomever purchased it.

He rejected the thought, however, knowing he had no desire to go into the city. He had been twice before to sell his work, and he had not enjoyed the experience either time. No, he would rather take the lower but still considerable price he could demand from one of the minor nobles in the valley. It would be sufficient for his needs. He didn't even consider taking it to an elven settlement, especially Caalenor; the idea of communing with his own kind felt like a betrayal of those he had lost.

Thus decided, Altoneir carefully wrapped the finished necklace in the soft fabric and placed it carefully back into his pack. Finally extinguishing the elven light, he lay on his blankets, his back stretching comfortingly after so long hunched over his work. As his body relaxed, he finally allowed his mind to fully return to visions of his mate, this time forcing himself to see her as she had been in life rather than how she had been in death, radiant and content as she smiled at him from across their table in the roundhouse. This time, he smiled softly as he imagined the jewel on her, smiled in a remembrance that somehow wasn't as painful as it had been before. He fell asleep more peacefully than he had since the avalanche, secure in the knowledge that the next day would begin his life anew.

Before the sun rose, he woke with a start, panting and sweaty. The vision of Aenwyn, her mouth open and stuffed with snow, had pulled him from his sleep once again. And, as it had been since her death, that image was the one that chased him as he packed his belongings and moved into the valley.

FURY

Though the daytime remembrances got easier, the nightmares of Aenwyn never really ceased as Altoneir trod southeast through the valley toward the old settlement of Y'Sathemar. He knew it was now a human village ruled over by two minor nobles distantly descended from the house of Agelon, which had existed since humans had come to Ilbeor. He had never traded with them, however, having never had a desire to visit his old home and see what had become of it.

Now, as his daytime visions of Aenwyn had become more beautiful than devastating, Altoneir wanted to see where they had once lived, feeling an inexplicable pull toward the very place he had avoided for centuries. He wanted to see if they had left the round-houses standing or razed them to build new human houses; he wanted to see if the home he had shared with Aenwyn still stood. Built to last, he knew the houses would have stood the test of time had the humans wanted them to, but humans were capricious creatures who did not always understand what they had been given. He hoped, at least, that the watchtower was still there; it would do him good to see one of those bastions of elvendom still standing after the destruction of the one in Shaamel.

Altoneir cursed softly as the light spring rain he had been traveling through deepened to a downpour, the wind heralding a storm on the horizon. That was one thing he had forgotten about the valley; if you were traveling, there were few places to find shelter from the weather. After a brief debate with himself and a quick analysis of the bend of the grasses as the storm approached, Altoneir decided the best thing to do was to keep walking. All stopping would do would be to force him to sit or kneel on the increasingly muddy ground in an effort to keep his head covered and, really, what use was there in that?

He kept as steady a pace as he could as the wind rose, blowing straight at him from the southeast and whipping his long black hair out of its leather thong. He told himself he didn't mind the chilled raindrops; he told himself the experience was cleansing and purifying, like somehow the droplets could wash his soul pure from his grief. In reality, however, he knew that all the rain was doing was soaking him to his very bones, running into his face and eyes from his sodden hair, and causing his robes to cling to him uncomfortably.

For perhaps fifteen minutes, the storm raged in full before diminishing to a light rain, and then to a drizzle. Still Altoneir walked on, knowing there would be no drying himself and his clothing until the rain had fully ceased and viewing the exercise as an antidote to the chill that had overtaken him. It was almost evening by the time the weather finally cleared to dryness, and Altoneir took the opportunity to not only dry himself and his clothing, but the items near the top of his traveling pack that had not escaped the downpour, either.

Just as he had decided to stop for the night, he heard voices - and the sound of them filled him with a joy he could not fully explain other than to note how very long it had been since he had experienced the companionship of anyone, be they elf or human. Looking around, he spotted the light of a campfire not far to his left; he had only failed to notice it because the light had not yet dimmed to twilight. The two human men he saw there belied all his prejudices by inviting him to share their fire and their meal, saying they welcomed the opportunity to get to know an elf for the first time in their lives.

After Altoneir had introduced himself, his use of Ilbeor's common tongue flawless despite his lack of recent practice, and settled himself by their rather large campfire on a clear space that had obviously been used as a camp before, he asked, "Where do you hail from, humans?"

The man on his left, Milon, middle-aged and portly with curly gray hair and a grizzled beard, laughed. "That's a new one," he guffawed. "Don't think I've ever been accused of being human before. What about you, Alec? You ever been called such a thing?"

Altoneir frowned. "But you are - "

Milon clapped him on the back hard enough that Altoneir rocked forward. The gesture felt completely foreign to Altoneir, for elves preferred a soft touch. Being essentially hit by this man startled him, but his discomfort was short-lived as Milon interrupted, "I know what I am, elf. But ya' see, people don't just go around calling each other 'human', and I ain't never met anyone from the other races, see, so it's strange to hear."

Altoneir tried not to let his confusion at the man's jovial attitude show; though he had dealt with humans on and off for centuries, he had never met one so informal and casual around him. "I see," he said finally. "My question stands, though. Where is your home?"

The man on his left, Alec, grinned at Altoneir. "We hail from Basendale, to the south there," he said, pointing. "We're traveling north to ford the river and see what there is to see to the north. We ain't married and got no children, so we're in the wind now our professions have been passed off to our apprentices."

The sheer amount of information Alec volunteered shocked Altoneir even further. Why would the man tell a stranger so much about his life, much less one not of his own race?

"What about you?" Milon asked. "Where do you come from, and what are ya doing here in the valley? Ain't your kind supposed to stay in the mountains?" He asked with a simple, open curiosity rather than with the suspicion and defensiveness Altoneir had half expected.

He was glad humans didn't have sharp enough hearing to notice the increase in his heart rate at the question. After considering for only half a moment, he decided he would not share news of Shaamel with these humans; what right had they to the knowledge, and why would they even care? Instead, he said, "I travel from the Chilpar Mountains on my way to Isasari, and then to the Gray Hills."

Milan whistled softly. "That's quite a journey to take alone, elf," he said, and Altoneir was amused at the man's insistence to say the name of his race in almost every comment after his surprise when Altoneir had called them humans. "Don't ya have family or friends to journey with?"

"No."

Alec and Milon looked at each other, and Altoneir could almost feel the shift in their bearings as they tried to divine the reason behind his curt reply. Still, he offered no further information, even as his memories tried to claw their way to the surface.

Alec finally broke the silence. "Well," he said, clapping his hands on his knees, "You can't get much finer eating than the venison we have with us, eh, Milon?" He indicated the meat sizzling over the fire, now appearing to be almost done. Altoneir, though he had supped well on the animals he had killed, felt his mouth water as he saw the green flecks of herbs rubbed on the meat and even thought he glimpsed the light shimmer of salt.

"I would be happy to dine with you, if you will still have me," Altoneir said.

Alec clapped him on the back again, the gesture still startling and foreign, but Altoneir didn't protest the treatment. "Have you?" he said, his voice booming across the valley. "Why, o'course we'll have you. Not often us humans get to share food with one of your kind."

Milon busied himself with the spit, taking the sizzling meat off it and cutting it into three pieces, which he put onto light metal plates.

The venison reminded Altoneir so strongly of home that at first, he had to work to swallow the pieces. The men had seasoned and cooked it to perfection, and it seemed less a camp meal and more something any of them could have expected in the comfort of their own homes and kitchens.

Alec watched him, not seeming to notice the emotion welling in his eyes or, more likely, misunderstanding it. "Good, ain't it?" he asked. "Milon here's as good a cook as ever was, though sometimes he slows us down collectin' things on the journey to add to the meat."

Milon grunted around his own mouthful of venison. When he had swallowed, he said, "You shouldn't complain, Alec. Without all those things, our meals wouldn't taste as they do. You like unseasoned meat?"

Altoneir thought of all the unseasoned meat he had eaten on his journey here and inclined his head at the man, acknowledging the truth of his statement.

Alec chuckled, and they continued the meal as they enjoyed light conversation. By the end, Altoneir thought he had misjudged humans in general: these men were amiable, intelligent, and had a wanderlust fairly common among the elves, though Altoneir himself didn't have that quality.

They are not so different from us.

Though the men's manner of speaking differed from the more measured, carefully courteous speech of the elves, he found the banter surprisingly refreshing. It was nice to be around people who were not constantly speaking of things of great import; no, conversation with Alec and Milon had been easy and enjoyable.

Perhaps, Altoneir thought, *I shall make my home in the valley among these people.*

He found the thought was not as repugnant as he had once imagined it to be.

ALTONEIR SURVEYED the patch of greenery, blossoming with an umbrella of small white flowers, growing among the grasses of the valley just north of the village that had once been Y'Sathemar. He missed Aenwyn for an entirely different reason than he had up to that point: in their partnership, she had been the one who best knew the plant life of the forest and, he was sure, the valley. She had needed to know for her work as a healer, but more than that, she had enjoyed knowing the uses of the flora and fauna around them.

She would have known if this would be something good to season meat.

Ever since his meal with Milon and Alec, Altoneir had kept himself alert for plant life to season his own meat and possibly even wild root vegetables or berries to add to his meals. Milon had kindly given him a small container of salt, refusing the coin Altoneir offered him for it, and he had used it sparingly ever since. But try as he might, Altoneir was just not talented in the way of identifying the various plants. He thought the growth at his feet might be thyme or something similar, but he only had a vague memory of something Aenwyn had used.

Deciding he would try it, Altoneir bent to tug up some of the greenery to add to his evening's meal. To his surprise, it resisted his tug, holding fast to the ground. It was stronger than it appeared.

Determined this plant would not best him, Altoneir tugged harder after loosening the soil a bit at the base of the plant. To his great surprise and honest delight, his efforts yielded not thyme, but a wild carrot, so pale yellow as to appear almost white amidst the dark soil that clung to it. Bringing it to his nose, he sniffed at it, wanting to ensure it was what he thought it was. The sweet, green scent that greeted his nose was all the confirmation he needed, and he grinned in spite of himself before beginning to unearth the rest of the roots. He thought that night's meal, what with the carrots, the flying squirrel he had hunted that morning, and the welcome addition of Milon's salt, would feel like a feast.

He purposefully camped far enough away from the former settlement of Y'Sathemar that he couldn't see it, for he knew once he did, he would feel an irresistible tug to enter. The human villagers were not likely to take kindly to an elven visitor so late in the evening, and he wanted his visit to go well and for the humans to respond to him in the same friendly manner Milon and Alec had.

The meal was truly a feast: spitting the fatty meat of the flying squirrel, which had been killed mercifully without a mark on its small body, above a makeshift oven of stones over the fire, Altoneir ensured that the grease from the meat would drip onto the carrots as they cooked. After seasoning it all with salt and some rosemary he had found earlier in the day, he sat by the fire, content to wait while the food cooked.

Altoneir sipped from his waterskin contemplatively, looking forward to some wine or possibly ale when he visited the human village tomorrow. Water slaked his thirst, but the relative tastelessness of it didn't satisfy in the way a good wine, ale, or spirit did. He wondered again what the dwellings would be like and whether the humans had kept the elven structures or razed them upon taking possession of the settlement.

He hoped they had kept them, and that they had cared for them well enough that they would still be standing. The stone structures of the elves were durable in all climates, but occasionally the mud-and-straw mortar had to be replenished or the stones cleaned of the moss wont to grow on them in damp places.

A shudder went through him as he thought of visiting the round-house he had shared with Aenwyn at the beginning of their mating, and a less poignant but still strong one went through him at the secondary thought of visiting his family's old hall. He knew, of course, that the dwellings would have been repurposed and he would find them much altered from the way they had been, but even just seeing them, just breathing the same air he had breathed in those happier times, appealed to him with an intensity he didn't entirely understand.

The gamey meat of the fat squirrel looked perfect with its dusting of salt and rub of rosemary, and Altoneir removed it from the spit, placing it carefully on his plate along with the carrots, now clean and trimmed and looking to burst with flavor. Cutting and spearing the first piece with his knife, he fought a groan of pleasure as he bit down on the juicy meat. It was almost as good as Milon's venison had been, and when he added a bite of sweet carrot, a flood of memories washed over him.

Aenwyn, who had cooked most of their meals, placing a porcelain plate in front of him, smiling gently.

Aenwyn, talking to him of her hopes for her spring garden as they sipped spiced wine and eaten of winter pork paired with orange sweet potatoes from the winter stores.

Aenwyn, her mouth full of -

He stopped the image short, choosing the cling to the more pleasant visions of their many shared meals over the centuries. He didn't wish to imagine the vision that still haunted his dreams, and he had become better at staving it off during the daylight hours.

When his meal was done, Altoneir took his plate to the stream near his camp and rinsed it and his knife in the cool, rushing water. As he returned to his fire and placed them back in his pack, he wished he had the supplies to ply his craft under an elven light in the dark night.

Blue. The next gemstone should be a rich blue, a sapphire to be cut into small pieces to fleck a silver setting like the night sky, interspersed with opal to represent the stars. The piece came into his mind's eye with a completeness all too familiar to him. It was the first time since he had left Shaamel that the vision of his future work had come to him just as it had in his workshop, and he relished the feeling of purpose and hope it gave him.

As soon as I sell the diamond, I will travel to Kol Todur and purchase what I need for it, he thought as he nestled himself into his blankets to await the dawning of the day that would finally take him to his ancient home. Though he knew his sleep would not be uninterrupted by nightmares, he still felt content as he drifted off, finally gleaning a direction in which his life might go - a direction in which he might yet find purpose.

ALTONEIR READ the runes on the small wooden sign at the side of the road to Y'Sathemar…not Y'Sathemar, but Faehill. He couldn't help but snort; there were no fae in Ilbeor, though there had been in the lands he had lived in before the Crossing. Faehill. What an utterly ridiculous name for a village.

Looking toward the town, Altoneir felt a thrill go through him as he realized almost all the original structures of Y'Sathemar remained standing, though the stone watchtower leaned slightly. Some roundhouses had been overtaken with vines, and there were the usual rectangular human dwellings among them, but the settlement he remembered was still there. He couldn't see the home he had shared with Aenwyn from where he stood, but he felt confident it was standing…and that he would soon be able to gaze upon it.

Altoneir pulled the hood of the cloak up onto his head, covering his long hair and his pointed ears. He hoped to escape detection upon his first look at the village. He wanted an opportunity just to take it all in. Perhaps if they couldn't really see him, they would think he was just an ordinary human traveler headed for the inn.

Perhaps I really will stay at the inn.

The thought surprised him; he hadn't stayed at a human inn for fifty years, since the last time he had come to the valley to sell his jewelry. He rarely enjoyed the experience, though it was somewhat better than sleeping in the outdoors. Steeling himself, Altoneir strode into the village.

The first thing he noticed as he entered, aside from the elven buildings still standing, was the everyday bustle of life in Faehill. The humans, not particularly noting his presence, went about their mornings briskly, seeming content enough with their lives. As he neared the village center, a group of three children dashed across his path so suddenly he had to halt himself to keep from being knocked into.

"Watch it there, trav'ler!" the oldest among them called over his shoulder, all three of them laughing uproariously at the close call.

When he reached the village square, Altoneir finally stopped. Unstrapping his pack from his back, he set it under the lone oak tree in one corner of the square, leaning it against the considerable trunk.

This was where the settlement circle used to be, he thought, surveying the area. Though the space was simply a flat square of spring green, a water well at one corner of it and the oak tree in the other, in his mind's eye he saw the depressed meeting place common to the elves, the place where they had come each evening to gather, hear news, and be entertained. The oak tree, though it seemed at least a century old by the breadth of its trunk, had not been here when he had lived here.

Altoneir moved to a place on the left side and stood, gazing into the center. He had taken the place where he and Aenwyn had usually sat, and though the view differed greatly from what it had been, he swore he could almost feel her shoulder brushing against his as they listened to the nightly music from the settlement songmaster.

"Can I help you, stranger?" The female voice, lower pitched than usual, startled him out of his reverie, and he looked around to see a woman dressed in a drab, brown woolen dress balancing a young baby on her hip.

Altoneir took a moment to recover himself before giving the answer he had prepared before he came to the village. "I am just passing through," he said. "I will seek lodging at the inn after I have taken a walk and gathered some supplies."

He had thought the answer would satisfy the curiosity of anyone who asked, but something about the way he looked or perhaps the way he had spoken seemed to alert the woman that he was not the normal type of traveler to come through the village. She peered at him, absently patting her baby's bottom as it fussed softly.

"Where're you from?" she asked finally, her voice still friendly but with an edge of suspicion.

Altoneir decided then and there to be honest with the woman and anyone else who crossed his path here. He could not hide what he was for long, and though elves could not dwell in the valley without permission from the royals, there was no law against them being there. He removed his hood from his head, shaking out his hair slightly, and said, "I hail from the settlement of Shaamel in the Chilpar Mountains. This village was once my home, and I thought to see it as I traveled to the Gray Hills."

The woman smiled at him, seeming to relax entirely now she had divined his true nature. "Very well, then," she said, moving the baby to her other hip. "Welcome to Faehill, stranger. We don't see many elves in these parts, but I'm sure you'll find us a welcoming people. The inn's just off the square over there." She pointed to the right with her free hand, and Altoneir's heart skipped a beat as he recognized the building she indicated as his family's hall, though a second story had been added, the beams of the wood it was constructed of contrasting oddly with the stone of the main structure.

Remembering his company, Altoneir inclined his head at her, doing his best not to appear affected by the sight. The woman nodded back and moved on, taking her baby into what appeared to be a bakery on the square.

Deciding he wasn't ready to see what the humans had done to his family's hall, Altoneir walked at an increasing pace, noting the combination of round and rectangular dwellings and buildings as he passed. He didn't like the contrast; somehow, the addition of these rectangular wooden human homes seemed vulgar to him, a disturbance to the tranquility Y'Sathemar had once exuded.

The next human he came across, a middle-aged man Altoneir guessed to be a blacksmith by the thick, meaty build of his arms and chest and the black apron he wore, greeted him with far more suspicion than the young mother had in the square. "What's your business here, elf?"

The question was edged with the hostility he had originally expected from the humans of the valley, and Altoneir immediately noted the demeanor that was so different from what he had encountered from Milon and Alec. The old hatred flared in him again, though he kept it hidden as he answered smoothly, "I am simply a traveler passing through."

The man crossed his arms, and Altoneir could not tell if the subsequent flexing of his biceps was intentional or simply a byproduct of his positioning. "Your kind don't belong here," he stated staunchly. "We live simple lives, and *your* place is in the mountains, far removed from the likes of us."

My place was taken from me.

Altoneir did not bother to hide his scowl, though he kept other signs of his rising temper in check. He did not feel threatened by this human, but by the same token, neither did he want a confrontation in this place. "I am simply passing through," he repeated, though he allowed a bit of an edge to creep into his voice this time. Let this man see just a hint of the predator lurking inside of him.

The stranger, to his credit, did not immediately back down when he noted the dangerous flash of Altoneir's eyes. Openly glaring, he made a final demand before stepping out of Altoneir's path. "Pass through, then, elf."

Altoneir felt the man's gaze burning into his back as he traversed the remaining distance to the roundhouse he had shared with Aenwyn as they had begun their lives together. When he reached it, however, his awareness of the hostile stranger faded into nonexistence.

The roundhouse in Y'Sathemar, like the one in Shaamel, was on the outskirts of the settlement; he and Aenwyn had always preferred to live some distance from the central lives of their communities. He supposed he should not have been surprised that no humans inhabited the old structure, but as he gazed upon what was left of his former home, he felt nothing more than the familiar rage from the forest, the fury he had thought had been tamed upon entering the valley's safety and tranquility.

Unlike the elven homes that had been put into use by the humans in the village, the more remote home Altoneir and Aenwyn had shared looked like it might not have been occupied even once in the centuries since they had left. And as he looked at its remains, he thought he would have rather they destroyed it, or at least just let nature take its course, than what they had done.

They had pillaged it. Over years, perhaps centuries, the people of Faehill had used his home to supply their other wants. The thatched roof, which of course would have needed care and replacement over the years, was entirely gone, leaving the inside of the structure open to the elements. And the house itself - the stones had been taken one by one, it seemed, and in a fashion that suggested the takers had simply pulled from whatever was closest, loosest, or easiest to access. Some parts of the rounded outer walls were peppered with gaping holes so large he could see through to the other side, while other parts remained more whole with only single stones missing, seemingly at random. The stone fireplace and chimney had collapsed into piles of rubble covered in weeds and moss, and where the stout wood-and-iron door had once been, only a broken archway remained.

And the garden - the garden Aenwyn had loved and presided over, caring for her vegetables, herbs, and flowers as though they had been her children - had not just been overrun by nature, but used as a receptacle for broken tools and pottery, the detritus of centuries of greedy, wasteful humans.

Altoneir felt his magic crackling at his fingertips, though he had no memory of actually summoning it. He wanted to destroy this desecration; he wanted to turn it to ash and dust so no other human could profit from his home; he wanted to ward the entire area so no human could ever step foot in it again.

Just as he raised his hands, the ball of destructive magic forming between them, he heard a small gasp from somewhere behind him. The sound drew him out of his noxious thoughts just long enough for the magic to dissipate as he turned to find the source of the sound. A child, no more than four years old by the look of him, stood alone in the space between the roundhouse and the village proper. Wearing a tunic of unbleached linen much too large for him and a pair of brown pants with frayed edges, the child looked as though he hadn't bathed in weeks.

Altoneir lowered his hands and surveyed the young boy, somewhat confounded by his appearance, alone and so far from the rest of the villagers, looking like he had not been cared for. Elven children were attended to with the utmost regard for their youth and the relative frailty of their minds and bodies, and though he had certainly encountered his share of raucous human children when he had ventured into the valley to sell his wares, he had never met one so young, so alone, and so woebegone.

"Where is your mother, child?" he asked, his voice harsher than he had intended it to be.

The child didn't answer him but continued to look at Altoneir's hands as though wondering where the red light had gone.

"Go," Altoneir ordered him, not liking the unblinking stare and distinctly uncomfortable with the boy's appearance.

Without making a single sound, the child turned and ran on dirty, bare feet back toward the village. Altoneir watched him go, frowning. Such a fragile young life, so easily warped or extinguished; he could have killed the child with half a thought. He wondered what guidance the child had at all, if it was left to wander alone at such an age. For where did reason and wisdom come from if not from the parents?

Alone again before the ruins of his former home, Altoneir's mind flashed to the last afternoon he and Aenwyn had spent together, to the child they had tried so desperately to create together. The child who would have been raised with such love and care...

That life is forfeit, he thought, and he wasn't certain if he was thinking of the sundered future of his own family or the uncertain fate of the bedraggled human child.

He forced his thoughts back onto the ruin before him, the ruin that seemed to symbolize everything his life had become, and the root cause of it: human hubris and greed.

This is *mine*, he thought with a finality that disregarded the terms of the treaty made so long ago. This place may have been destroyed by generations of the filthy humans who had stolen it and everything else he had held dear, but it was *his*. And he no longer wanted to destroy it; he wanted to reclaim it.

For her, I will rebuild this home. For her, I will dwell here. For her, I will bring the garden to life once again.

Filled with a purpose that just overtook the anger coursing through him, he turned from the wreckage of his former home and stalked back into the village, his stride long and his face set with determination.

"IT'S NOT POSSIBLE." Jurdan, the first person the shopkeeper had directed him to when he had requested an audience with one of the village elders, leaned back in the wooden chair he occupied in the village hall. "We don't want an elf living here, and it's not your place, anyway. Your place is the mountains, as it always has been. By royal decree, elves are not to dwell in the valley but by special edict. Do not make the mistake of thinking I won't call in the King's guard to remove you if need be."

"Our place has not always been in the mountains," Altoneir pointed out, a dangerous edge to his voice as his patience rapidly frayed. "The very buildings you dwell in were built by my people, some of them by my very hands, including the one that lies in ruins on the outskirts." He felt he had been very clear on this point and on his purpose, and Jurdan's threat of calling the royal guard to eject him from his former home infuriated him.

But for this edict he is so proud of, Aenwyn would still be alive.

Altoneir tempered his fury, concealing it from the smug human sitting across from him. Jurdan, who Altoneir guessed to be past his seventieth year by the frailty of his body and his long, white hair, seemed utterly sure of his authority in this matter and seemed adamant against listening to any of Altoneir's reasoned arguments.

"The buildings were ceded to us as part of the treaty," Jurdan said inexorably. "You have no claim upon them, elf, and no threat of magic and heresy will grant you that claim."

"I have threatened no magic, nor have I spoken heresy." The utter lack of emotion in the statement should have alerted Jurdan to the danger he faced, but the man remained inexorable.

"And what does a traveler who comes with nothing offer this village? We need no beggars."

Red tinged the edges of Altoneir's vision, but he once again denied himself the luxury of displaying the rage that grew with this human's every word. His voice carefully measured in the way that only an elf could manage, he said, "I do not ask for charity. My profession would bring wealth to this community, and I would patronize every shop and craft in the village for my own needs. I could supply magical aid if it was called for. My residence in this village would be an asset, not a liability." The words, while an utter misrepresentation of Altoneir's purposes, were carefully crafted to appeal to the innate greed of humanity.

Perhaps the way to reclaim what is mine is through offerings of peace and wealth.

Jurdan stood, ignoring Altoneir's argument with a superior sort of disdain that again made his magic crackle at the end of his fingertips. "This meeting has ended," he declared. "You have my answer, elf. You may stay in the inn tonight if you wish, but I expect you gone by tomorrow noon."

Altoneir stood so quickly the movement seemed instantaneous, and he saw a flash of fear cross Jurdan's face as his rage fully consumed him and he lifted his hands, the red light of his battle magic having already manifested. The room shifted in that moment, in that eternity between one heartbeat and the next, for instead of a frail, elderly human, Altoneir saw only a monster without a soul, saw only the reason for the sundering of his world.

Jurdan's scream was so high-pitched it rang in Altoneir's ears after it abruptly cut off. He gazed at the human who had denied him his right to live in safety and peace, now lying on the wooden floor of the village hall with his guts hanging out of his body, gasping for air as tears of pain ran down his face. His obvious fear and horror did nothing to temper Altoneir's rage, and he decided then and there that he would not offer this human the mercy of a quick death.

Altoneir heard footsteps running from the outside; no doubt, the other human vermin of the village had heard Jurdan's cry and come to investigate the source. He didn't wait for them to enter the hall. Rather, he kicked the door open, his battle magic still raging between his hands, and faced them head on as they thundered up the three wooden steps to the building.

Altoneir saw the fear and confusion on the humans' faces as he stared them down. They had no weapons, having not realized there would be any need for them, but it wouldn't have mattered if they had. Without taking even a moment to temper his fury, Altoneir cut them down one by one, his slashing movements quick and practiced from his many kills in the forest as he had traveled. Six bodies littered the area in front of the hall in less than a minute's time, and he heard yet another scream as he looked up from his kills.

The woman he had talked to before, the one with the baby, stood with two other female villagers and a small herd of children on the edge of the square.

Altoneir knew what they saw: six bodies, but more than that, himself - not only holding battle magic in his hands but surrounded by an aura of it, a red aura that would make him seem to pulse with the very power he carried.

"Go," he ordered, his voice booming. "Go."

The women ran, calling for the children to follow them. Moments later, the square was clear again, at least until someone else saw what he had done.

Altoneir didn't care. He strode through the village, that red aura pulsing, and flung his magic at the pathetic wooden human dwellings, leaving the elven dwellings in peace. Fire sprang up in his wake, and people poured onto the streets, fleeing their burning homes and coming to investigate the source of the disturbance to their usually tranquil lives.

Three men, burly and younger than the ones he had seen before, blocked his path, each holding a weapon of some sort. Altoneir stopped in front of them and stared into each of their eyes, letting his power show itself plainly.

"Stop, you!" one man called bravely.

Altoneir said nothing and did not move. He would have them all dead in a matter of moments no matter what they tried to do with their rusted pitchforks and kitchen knives, but he enjoyed watching as the righteous, protective anger faded from their eyes, to be replaced by fear as they stared at the inexorable elf standing before them, the killing light resting in a crackling ball between his hands.

Yes, fear me. You should fear all of us from whom you took safety and security for your own gain.

Tiring of the standoff, Altoneir sent the cutting magic at each of them, neatly removing their heads from their shoulders before they had so much as made a move toward him.

After that, no one challenged him as he stalked through the village, burning every human dwelling he came across until he at last came full circle back to the inn and its ramshackle addition to what had been his family's hall.

The innkeeper, a rotund man with a grizzly beard like Milon's, stood in front of it, but he made no move to challenge Altoneir as Altoneir set the upper story of his inn ablaze, not caring if it ended up damaging the lower story as well. The stones of his family's hall should be able to withstand the fire if the humans put it out quickly, but he found he didn't care if they did or did not. These humans did not deserve to live in his family's hall, to use it for their own drinking and carousing.

A woman and four children, all under the age of ten by the looks of them, dashed out of the inn as the fire took shape. Behind them, a ragtag group of travelers, mostly men, followed.

"Please," the woman gasped. "Please, spare my children."

Altoneir kept with his method of staring them down without saying a word, but he decided not to attack the group even though it contained many fully grown men. Without breaking his stare at the innkeeper and his family, he dropped his hands to his sides, the battle magic winking out as though it had been nothing more than an elven light.

He turned, aware that every eye on the village was on him and that they were all full of fear as he strode out of the village. He looked like nothing more than a traveler then, with his pack and his cloak on his back, but no one was foolish enough to approach him.

As he reached the edge of the village, Altoneir turned to take one last look at the buildings that had once comprised Y'Sathemar and the humans who now dwelled there. The plumes of smoke from the human structures pleased him, as did what he imagined to be the stench of fear in the air from all those who watched him go.

He wanted them to fear him, and fear his eventual return, for the rest of their miserable lives.

FOUND

Altoneir would never forget, nor did he think he could ever replace, the complete satisfaction he had felt upon walking away from Faehill knowing the humans there would fear him for the rest of their lives. The satisfaction came from knowing that he had taken away a big component of the safety and peace humans had stolen from the elves when the treaty was forged…a big component of the safety and peace he himself had been denied when the smug village elder had denied his petition to live there as one of them.

They must not be allowed immunity from what they have done, what they took away.

He once again cursed the ancient elven elders who had forged the treaty to live peacefully with the human race; he once again thought scornfully of their unwillingness to use their magic to defend what was theirs. Peace was a noble pursuit, to be sure, but what of safety and protection of their own?

As he continued through the valley, heading vaguely toward the Gray Hills and Kol Todur, the small city where the dwarves mined and sold the gems and silver he used in creating his jewels, Altoneir found small resurgences of that feeling of power and satisfaction when he hunted the animals along his way. Whether rabbits, squirrels, or larger game like deer, he found something akin to delight in the rush of killing them painfully, killing them in a way that would cause them fear.

When he reached the foothills of the mountain range that would take him to his goal, he stopped with no prior planning in a large clearing in the trees, close enough to the edge of the valley that he might still access the human lands with ease, but far enough back to hide himself within the cover of the mountain forest. Despite his complete lack of thought about where he might make a permanent home, the place struck him as somewhere he could dwell alone and in peace, somewhere he might forge a new life separate from anything or anyone who might disturb him.

Deciding to stop and make camp though it was barely an hour into the afternoon, Altoneir set to work in a way he hadn't with his previous camps. Instead of simply clearing enough space to make his small campfire and lay out his blankets, he set his pack down and began clearing the brush and forest detritus from the entire area. Even using magic, the process took quite some time: it was clear no one had ever taken pains with the clearing before, and some roots of the brush ran deeper than he would have expected. Still, however, he was finished before the sun had truly begun to set, and he surveyed the area with the eye of one considering a new settlement.

The area was wide; he thought it perhaps a hundred feet across and half over that in depth, the slope of it gentle enough he knew he could build a permanent dwelling there if he wished. He also thought, with a pang of longing and remembrance for his mate, that he could make a small garden there, given time.

Deciding he would stay at least for the time being, Altoneir set to work to create the first shelter he had bothered with since leaving Shaamel, an angled canopy of bough and brush held up by two wooden poles. When he wasn't able to finish it before dark fell, he set three elven lights in the clearing and continued by their light and that of his small fire.

As he worked into the night, Altoneir thought of the fevered pace at which he had finished the diamond pendant in the valley, working under an elven light just as he was doing tonight. With an abruptness that startled him, he realized he might stave off the nightmares that still plagued him by working in the darkness, and getting what sleep he needed in the morning's light.

At the thought, though his hands were still busy with lashing the boughs of his shelter, the all-to-familiar vision of Aenwyn at the time of her death flashed into his mind, and his hands immediately ceased their work. He barely noticed the clamor of the bough falling to the clearing floor as he gasped for air, not able to vanquish the vision however much he might have wanted to.

Her eyes...her eyes were so empty...and she couldn't breathe.

Altoneir could never decide which part of the vision was worse: the memory of her mouth packed with snow, or the memory of those beautiful eyes bereft of light.

Trying to shake it off but not succeeding for several minutes, Altoneir abruptly decided that, though he had some leftover meat in his pack, he wanted to go on a night hunt. Though he had never done so before, he had heard from the hunters of Shaamel that to do so was a challenge that called every sense you possessed into play. Perhaps it would be just what he needed to banish the night's visions.

Leaving his unfinished shelter behind, Altoneir stalked quietly into the forest surrounding the clearing, stopping to give his eyes and senses time to adjust to the darkness once he had gone beyond the reach of his firelight. Listening carefully, he thought he heard the lap of a tongue against a body of water some distance away and, thinking he would not only find prey but fresh water, he kept his footfalls as silent as possible and used his elven vision and hearing to track the noise.

The wolf must have been fresh from a kill of its own, for as it lapped at the water in the small forest pond a short distance from Altoneir's camp, its muzzle was dark with what smelled like fresh blood. The creature was magnificent; large and well-muscled, it had obviously fed well since winter, its long gray fur seeming to gleam in the moonlight.

It looked up from the pond and, seeing Altoneir, lowered itself into a crouch, showing its teeth and growling. Altoneir smiled at it, a smile that rose to whatever challenge the wolf was preparing to pose.

He knew he could have killed it without uttering a word, without even raising his hand. But here, as he met the first real challenge he had faced since the *allihr*, he felt the urge to give the wolf a chance to fight if it so chose. He simply stood and watched it, no words on his lips, no magic between his hands.

The elf and the wolf studied one another for several long moments, the wolf never ceasing its low growl. Altoneir relished the sight of it, the blood drying on its muzzle, the yellow fangs on full display. Here was another predator, another force of nature to contend with, and he looked forward to actually using some skill against it.

He could tell the wolf was going to spring only a moment before it did; a slight shifting of its weight onto the crouching back legs, a slight raise of its snout, was all the warning the wolf gave. Altoneir let it come, watching it bound straight for him after leaping right over the small pond. Only when it was almost to him, teeth bared and mouth open, readying for the kill, did he move.

Instead of using magic, Altoneir used his elven strength to lash out with his hand even as he neatly stepped out of the wolf's path. The wolf yelped as it was knocked aside, though the blow wasn't hard enough to fell it. Immediately, it wheeled about and approached him again, this time stalking, seeming to try to find the best angle for the kill.

Only then did Altoneir allow the destructive red magic to bloom between his hands, but rather than flinging it immediately at the wolf, he simply held it in place, waiting to see what the animal would make of the new development, if it would sense its death in the light of Altoneir's magic.

Altoneir had to admit being impressed when the wolf did not hesitate for even a moment to examine the magic. It was a predator, just as he was, and it knew what it wanted. Futile though Altoneir knew its efforts were, he appreciated the majesty of the animal, nonetheless.

He finally struck, sending a spear of light right through the wolf's enormous eye, straight and strong as a master hunter's arrow. The wolf made no sound as it fell forward, its momentum carrying it several feet before it slid to a stop. Altoneir knew it was dead before it had hit the ground; he'd had no desire to torture or cause fear in this magnificent animal; its bravery was to be lauded, not punished.

Even with his elven strength, Altoneir had some difficulty heaving the large animal's body over his shoulders. The blood from his magical arrow, now winked out of existence, leaked from the wolf's vacant eye socket onto his robes as he strode back to his new home, well satisfied.

WITHIN A WEEK of deciding he was going to call the clearing his home for the time being, Altoneir had erected the slanted-roof shelter, spread his blankets and belongings under it, dug a pit for his fire in the middle of the area, and warded the entire thing so no scavengers or thieves could enter without his leave. The meat from the wolf proved to be only slightly more appetizing than the *allihr* had been, especially when Altoneir used some of his remaining salt and some gathered herbs in the cooking process. He found it to be too lean and tough, the odor stronger than what he had come to expect from other game.

Deciding after he had consumed three meals' worth of the meat that he would prefer to dine on more traditional food sources, he burned what was left of it, reserving the pelt to be traded or cured into a warm bed covering. Later that same day, he found a large patch of early-blooming hare's lemon, the vibrant yellow color calling attention to them amidst the flora and fauna of the forest. When Altoneir popped the first one into his mouth, the tart explosion of juices on his tongue felt like a taste of the home he had almost made himself forget. Hare's lemon had grown rampant around Shaamel in the late spring, and all the elves of the settlement had loved to gather them, both for the unique flavor of the berries themselves and the healing properties of the three-edged leaves.

Altoneir was careful not to completely strip the low-growing bramble of the berries; some needed to be left for the patch to propagate in future seasons, to spread and grow. He did, however, fill a large makeshift gathering pack with both the berries and the leaves, some to eat fresh, others to bake to a mushy tenderness that, when sweetened with sugar, made for a treat every elf greatly enjoyed.

Sugar. That was not something he would chance upon or be able to gather in the forests or the nearby valley; the grass-like canes only grew in the far north on the Steppes and had to be imported by everyone south of the humans' royal mountain.

The list of things he needed and wanted both for his craft and the new life he was trying to forge for himself grew each day, and he knew he could no longer put off the interaction with the other beings of Ilbeor. It was time to venture out, and woe betide anyone who refused him the safety and peace he was finally beginning to forge for himself.

Leaving his warded camp with not much in it but the shelter and the banked remains of the previous night's fire, Altoneir once again hefted his pack and set off on a journey, this time east and upward into the Gray Hills, the mountain range that bordered the Unforgiving Lands from which the dwarves were reputed to have come.

Altoneir somewhat enjoyed his travels for the first several days. The season was warming, the surrounding trees just different enough from his former home in the Chilpar Mountains to offer interesting sights as he traveled. He found small game with little effort, and he chanced upon another patch of hare's lemon as well as some various patches of mint and herbs soon after he set off.

The diamond pendant weighed heavily in the pocket of his travel-worn robes, where he had stowed it for safekeeping rather than keeping it buried in his pack. Though he was not overly worried about losing it and knew he could easily and gladly fend off any would-be bandits, he was also acutely aware that the diamond held his only hope and chance for survival as he wanted it: completely on his own. If he somehow didn't have it to sell when he reached Kol Todur or Gelrhia, the ancient dwarven capital city, he would have no choice but to join a community if for no other reason than he was not an adept enough wilderness survivalist to have any kind of life he would want to lead long-term.

On the fourth day, Altoneir wondered why he had met no humans or dwarves on the Gray Hills trails to Kol Todur. He had not tried to avoid the trodden trails, as he felt that his lack of the same intimate familiarity he'd had in the Chilpars might cause him to get lost on the game trails or off the trails altogether. He felt that, in the wholly pleasant season of the southeastern spring, he should have met many travelers on his way.

He found his answer on the fifth day after he had woken in the early light of pre-dawn and recommenced his journey. Before he had walked for even an hour, four gray-skinned monsters burst out of the brush to his right and left side, blue magic crackling between each of their long-fingered hands as they ambushed him for no other reason than the pleasure of the kill.

Shielding himself was instinctual, and his shield deflected the four balls of destructive magic they immediately sent his way even as he felt their impacts reverberate through his entire being. For a moment, even given the immediate danger of his situation, he was forced back into the avalanche, back into feeling the wall of snow barrel into his shield and toss him down the mountain.

Altoneir blinked away the memory, forcing himself to focus on the situation at hand. He felt the first genuine fear he had felt since the destruction of his settlement, a much more pervasive and long-lasting thing than the momentary jolt he had felt when the *allihr* had woken him.

The four creatures facing him were Urothu. Bald with small, beady black eyes, they were roughly the shape of a small elf, but they wore no clothing and their skin was a faded, sickly gray that reminded Altoneir of death in its very lack of color. Urothu had been in Ilbeor when elves had arrived in the Crossing, and even the dwarves and tselqs couldn't remember a time when they hadn't been there. More powerfully magical than all but the most powerful elves, Urothu seemed to have no purpose but killing and destruction and seemed to take a perverse sort of pleasure in it. Though they might pillage the belongings of the travelers they killed, they never ate the meat of two-legged or four-legged beings, simply leaving their destroyed bodies behind to rot. Almost no living being to encounter them had lived to tell the tale, and what knowledge there was of them only existed because the ancient elves had once captured one that was separated from its clan and held it captive long enough to study it before they killed it. The only thing they had concluded was that the Urothu was not a natural being - for no species known to anyone killed for the sake of killing.

As Altoneir gazed at the four Urothu staring him down through his transparent shield, their magic already crackling between their hands again, he knew his chances of survival were slim. If he kept his shield up, they would continue flinging their battle magic at it until it faltered, even if it took hours, even if it took days. If he let his shield down so he could attack them, he would have a matter of only a second or two to make the kills before their magic reached him.

I am more powerful than them.

He knew that with a certainty borne of years being one of the most powerfully magical elves on Ilbeor. His magic, when he chose to unleash it, contained a raw strength that transcended even his own physical body's limitations sometimes, as it had with the *allihr*. But strength would not be enough to win this battle; against four of them, speed and strategy were his only hope.

Four more powerful waves of magic hit his shield, but this time his mind did not wander as he carefully evaluated the strength and speed with which they would come. He had but one hope. If it failed, he would die.

Altoneir waited out the moment it took them to reclaim the magic and send it toward his shield again. At the last possible second, he dove to his left, bringing his shield down in time for the magic to soar above his head. Now, this heartbeat, was the only chance he had to survive.

Reaching towards them, Altoneir summoned every bit of power within himself and flung it in four elegant but brutal spears toward the creatures. He was out of his dive and in a crouch before he knew if they had hit their marks, but he knew that if they hadn't, the last thing he would see was blue magic hurtling toward him once again, this time with no shield to block it.

When nothing happened, he dared a glance. The four Urothu lay in a tangled heap in the middle of the path, each of their chests sporting a gaping hole seeping blood so purple it almost appeared black in the early morning light. Only one still breathed; only one chest continued to rise and fall as it raised its hands and summoned its magic with what Altoneir knew must be the last of its strength.

He stood stock still as he watched the creature rally, watched it raise its head from the forest floor to look at him with a gaze of unadulterated hate. Altoneir didn't shield or respond to the impending attack at first; he simply watched the gray-skinned Urothu summoned the wherewithal for one last attack. He knew the Urothu would soon die at his hands, and he wondered if it, too, sensed its own demise. Unlike with the wolf, he felt no sense of admiration for the Urothu - this final attempt was not borne of bravery and determination, but rather of the putrid psychopathy of its race.

He shielded just in time, having underestimated the time it would take the Urothu to rally. The magic reverberated against the shield as the other bolts had done, but it hit with a profound lack of the brutal strength of the ones before. Altoneir brought the shield down as he had before, dodging from the path of a second attempt even as he rallied his own magic for the kill.

His magical blade decapitated the remaining Urothu, cutting off even the slightest chance of further attack.

He loosed a long breath. Urothu rarely traveled in packs of more than three or four; it was rumored they killed even one another when they became too crowded. He wondered if these four had been wreaking havoc along this trail, if warnings had gone out to travelers not to come this way. He thought it was a good possibility.

Just as they would have done if they had won their short fight, he left the bodies lying right on the trail, simply stepping around them and continuing on his way. As he worked his way upward from the scene, the only aspect of him that hinted at the exertion of his efforts was his ragged breathing; his face remained calm, his eyes promising a painful death to anyone else who crossed his path.

ALTONEIR HOPED he would be able to sell the diamond in Kol Todur; Gelrhia was on the other side of the mountain and would have required weeks more travel. Having not met a soul on the trails after he had killed the Urothu, he arrived at the mining city late one morning.

He did not bother with any of the several inns in the city. He wished to conduct his business and leave the company of the dwarves, who he had never enjoyed conversing with. Instead, he went straight to the home of the mayor of Kol Todur, a dwarf who did no work with his hands or body and, as a result, was more rotund than average. Altoneir had dealt with him before and felt he would easily gain an audience.

He was not mistaken. After he had identified himself to the servant who had answered the door of the large stone house and she had conferred with her master, he was led through the sparsely adorned corridors to one of the sitting rooms at the back of the house.

Dwarves had the tendency to be austere in their home furnishings; though their mining and gem craft had brought the race much wealth, they hoarded it rather than spending it, believing there would be a time in the future when the dwarven race would need the vast stores of coin and jewels to survive. Altoneir only saw three pieces of decor as he followed the servant: two portraits of what he assumed were family ancestors, and a large hourglass sitting proudly in the front hall as he had entered.

The servant didn't announce him as they entered the room; that was not the dwarven way. Instead, she just bowed in what humans would have considered a male fashion and left, closing the door to the chamber behind her. In the middle of the room, on a cushioned chair built to hold his girth, sat Gravor Flintjaw and his wife, having been in the middle of a late afternoon repast of tea and biscuits before Altoneir had come.

With some difficulty, Gravor Flintjaw stood, though his wife remained seated. "Altoneir! Ysk, but it's good to see you. What have you brought for me today, eh? A trinket for my lovely wife, eh? Or perhaps a plaything for my children's children?" His voice was at once booming and gravelly, somehow seeming to defy his stature. When he stood at his full height, he barely reached Altoneir's waist, his ornate blue jacket and black pants appearing they had been made for a child but for the allowances made for his girth.

Altoneir didn't smile, but he inclined his head slightly, a sign of respect rather than reverence. This dwarf was no king, but merely a mayor. "Greetings, Gravor," he said smoothly, his voice betraying none of the discomfort or irritation he felt to be in the dwarf's company. "I think you will like what I have brought you today."

"So serious, our elven friend," Gravor commented to his wife. Then he turned once again to Altoneir. "Seat yourself, elf! The days of travel wear badly on you. We would never have expected to see you in our chambers looking as you do, eh? After our business here is done, Hendore must order you a bath."

Hendore Flintjaw, the wife of the mayor, suddenly laughed. "Don't mind this *kænsadr*, Altoneir." The mild profanity was not unexpected, even from a female, but Altoneir still fought rolling his eyes. "Come, sit, and tell us of your journey."

After unstrapping his pack from his back and setting it on the floor near the sitting area, Altoneir took the chair opposite Gravor and Hendore, almost sitting too hard in the low seat. As he had always done, he stretched his long legs somewhat to make himself as comfortable as possible as he sat on the chair meant for one half his stature.

"I met a band of Urothu on the trails," he announced, his voice almost bored.

Gravor exchanged a look with his wife. "We have heard of it," Gravor said, his voice less jovial than it had been before. "Bodies have been found on the trails these past months. We buried them as should be done, but we then sent an edict to use the northern trails to come this way. You did not hear of it, I think."

"I did not." Altoneir inclined his head again, acknowledging that he would have followed the order had he known of it.

"And yet here you sit, elf," Hendore said, her voice not much higher in pitch than her husband's. She fingered the fabric of her dark red velvet skirt, embroidered with mountain flowers.

"The Urothu did not survive the encounter," Altoneir said drily. "I think you will find that band will trouble the trails no more."

Gravor clapped his meaty hands together. "A job well done, elf! *Oskünr*! Those beasts have troubled our mountain more lately than ever before."

Hendore, seeming to see that Altoneir didn't wish to continue the line of conversation, asked, "You have brought us a trinket, eh?"

Altoneir did not show any sign of gratitude for the change in subject, but he reached into the pocket of his bedraggled brown robes and produced the blue fabric roll in which he had been keeping the diamond pendant. Without saying a word, he removed the piece and held it by its chain, displaying it. It rotated slowly, catching the afternoon light from the large glass windows, and Altoneir thought once again that it seemed to glow with its own fire.

As one, Gravor and Hendore stood and crossed the short distance to Altoneir's chair to examine it.

"I may touch it, eh?" Hendore asked after a moment.

"You may."

Hendore fingered the pendant, her small brown eyes seeming to reflect its glow. Though dwarves did not voice the same awe or appreciation humans often did at his work, he could tell she admired it.

"The diamond is one of Berfuth Redforge's, I think," Gravor said contemplatively as Hendore continued to examine the cut of the diamond and its delicate setting.

"It is," Altoneir confirmed. "He brought it to my settlement in the early fall with the traders. I found little reason to alter the cut."

Gravor's voice suddenly boomed again. "No reason to alter perfection, eh? That *grysk* cuts the diamonds in a way not keeping with our traditions, yet they come out better than anyone else's."

"The setting is not of our make," Hendore commented, her voice soft as she continued gazing at the pendant. "Master silversmiths we may have, but none who do the delicate work of these hands. Tell me, elf, who crafted this."

Altoneir thought of telling her he had crafted it himself, not from a desire to take credit, but to avoid having to speak of his father. But after a moment, he said, "My father, Ayduin."

"Recruit him to our silversmith's guild, I should!" Gravor exclaimed. "He could teach those asses a thing or two."

Altoneir made no comment, knowing that to share the death of his father would be to bring the memories washing down upon him once again. The fate of Shaamel had no bearing on their business here.

"I want it," Hendore said with certainty. She turned to her husband. "This would make a fine wedding gift for Hefraed and Bosasli. They could start their stores in earnest with such a gift, eh?"

"That they could, wife."

Hendore turned back to Altoneir. "You require a great price for such a piece, eh?"

Altoneir remembered that in dwarven families, it was the female who controlled the flow of coin rather than their husbands. He named a price that would have been sufficient to buy a small castle.

Hendore grunted, but not, Altoneir knew, because she thought his price unfair. Miserly the dwarves might be, but they knew the value of the craftsmanship and materials he had presented to them. She would not have expected the diamond to be sold for anything less than a small fortune. After a moment, she named another price, lower but not insultingly so.

Altoneir inclined his head at her. "I could sell this in Gelrhia or even Emelle for more than the price I originally named," he stated.

Hendore nodded in acknowledgement, but responded, "Yet you are not in Gelrhia or Emelle, eh? You are here, and you wish for a quick sale." Gravor remained silent during the exchange, amused at the careful negotiation taking place before him.

Altoneir named a price almost exactly halving the difference between his original offer and her response to it. He knew doing so would throw her off for at least a moment; she would have expected him to remain closer to his opening price.

Gravor chuckled, the deep amusement of it reverberating through the room. "The elf wishes to cut the negotiation short, wife," he observed.

"I do not need to bandy words," Altoneir said smoothly, not showing the irritation he was starting to feel. "The quality of what I offer is obvious, as is its value."

Hendore gazed at him, her eyes narrowed, wholly ignoring her husband. Altoneir knew this was the moment of truth, the moment in which she would either make an acceptable offer or withdraw completely. He would not yield further; if he had to travel to Gelrhia to obtain a fair price for the diamond, he would do so.

After a long moment, Hendore named a price only slightly lower than his latest offer, and Altoneir knew she did it more to feel as though the negotiation had gone in her favor than out of necessity. He kept his small smile of satisfaction to himself; she had behaved as he had predicted she would, and the price she had named was more than enough to supply his wants and needs for a very long time. "It is done," he said.

Hendore and Gravor both looked surprised, and Altoneir knew why: dwarves would negotiate for hours on something as fine as the diamond he still held in his hands. To them, the haggling was nearly as valuable as the object itself. To have the price agreed upon in only a few minutes upset their sensibilities.

Hendore inclined her head in agreement, nonetheless.

"In addition to the coin, I would parley with you." Altoneir had saved this statement for the point at which they had agreed upon a price. It wasn't a vital point; with the coin from the sale, he would easily have been able to purchase his required items himself, but he aimed to see just how much he could gain.

"*Oskünr,*" Gravor swore, though his face remained good natured. "I should have known you wouldn't name such a price without further parley, elf! Let's hear it, eh?"

"My wants are simple," Altoneir told him. "New robes made, four sets, two of linen and two of wool. A store of salt, herbs, and spices. A store of sugar and flour. Preserved meats and one fresh kill. Vegetables and fruits, some preserved, some fresh. A sturdy kitchen knife. I also have a wolf pelt I would trade for a cured fur."

"Simple, eh?" Hendore sounded amused. "And how do you propose to carry these supplies, elf? You brought no companions."

"Ah, yes. A handcart suited for the trails," Altoneir added as though he had forgotten to make the request, though in truth he had saved it for last to seal the bargain. He knew the dwarves made such carts just as the elves did, and though it would make his progress much slower, it would enable him to return to his clearing alone.

"It is done," Hendore declared, slapping her hands, bereft of jewelry but for a simple wedding band, on her skirts.

Handing over the diamond was an unexpected blow, for Altoneir suddenly felt he was giving the dwarves the last piece he had left of his mate. The picture he had once relished of Aenwyn smiling at him, the magnificent pendant hanging just above the cleft of her breasts, flashed into his mind as Hendore took both the diamond and its wrappings from him. He had to remind himself that the money and supplies were necessary to his survival, carefully avoiding thinking about the fact that Aenwyn could never wear the diamond, anyway.

When the deal was done, Altoneir left the grand but unadorned house and set about purchasing supplies from the gem and silver vendors in the markets of Kol Todur. By the time he had what he needed to work again, the purse he had received from Hendore Flintjaw was noticeably depleted, but this didn't worry him. He had what he needed to survive for quite some time, and he knew he would turn a considerable profit from the finished pieces he would create over the coming season.

With a grimace, he realized he would have to spend some nights at one of the inns while the dwarven seamstresses made his robes; they did not keep ready-made pieces for elves, unsurprisingly. He decided he would find something to read in either the inn's library or Gravor's and spend as much of the time as possible in his room, that he need not endure the noisy company of the dwarves in the city.

His robes were ready three days after his meeting with the mayor and his wife, and without so much as a goodbye or a glance behind him at the last settlement he would see for the foreseeable future, Altoneir hefted the handles of the full cart and made his way back down the trails to his new home in the clearing.

As ALTONEIR PULLED his laden cart into the clearing, he noted some differences immediately: the few belongings he had left behind had been disturbed, and his shelter had three fresh branches laid upon it, though in his opinion it had been fine the way it was.

He frowned, stopping his progress as he surveyed his new home. He had left only minimal wards around the place as he had departed, knowing the magic needed to sustain them would wane with his absence anyway and that he had left nothing of value behind. Honestly, he had expected no one to come that way in the first place; the worst he had expected was to find an animal nestled into his remaining blankets under the shelter, and that problem could have been easily dealt with it.

Setting the handles of the cart down, Altoneir strode into the clearing, his battle aura pulsing as red magic bloomed between his hands. "Who has come to this place?" he called, his voice deadly.

A rustling in the trees across the clearing caught his attention, and Altoneir snapped into an immediate offensive posture as two elves emerged, as familiar as they were unwelcome: Paeral and Inaadi. He didn't relax as they walked forward, their stances carefully non-threatening, their faces unreadable.

"Stand down, Altoneir," Paeral called. "I am certain you can see we mean you no harm."

"I had no wish to be followed," Altoneir responded, though he relaxed his posture and let the magic go.

"That much is clear enough, but the path of destruction you have wrought on your way here took almost no time to come to the attention of the elders in Caalenor. It seems the humans of Faehill sent a desperate call for aid by a horseback messenger." Paeral's voice was calm and held no hint of reprobation, but Altoneir still bristled at the words.

"Those humans had their chance to placate me," he said. "Their payment for denying my petition was nothing more than just."

"Denying your petition?" Inaadi asked, her thin eyebrows lifting. "What could you possibly have asked of humans to evoke such a response when you were refused? Did you call for aid against some danger? Were you on the brink of starvation?" She looked pointedly at Altoneir, who, while travel-worn, had certainly not lacked in nourishment since those early days in the forests of the Chilpar Mountains.

Altoneir did not answer.

Paeral spoke again. "We seek not to debate the past. What has been done, has been done. The elders cannot change the outcome of your grievance against the humans of Faehill and have no wish to punish what they were certain was an act of immeasurable grief. All we ask is that you come with us, to live among our kind again and find healing."

Altoneir could not restrain himself from his dark, bitter laugh. "Find healing?" he asked. "How do you, Paeral and Inaadi, presume to tell me to find healing when you stand next to one another, neither having lost your mate?"

Inaadi, though she remained as calm as ever, seemed to take some slight offense at his words. "We have suffered great losses as well, Altoneir," she said gently. "Though we have been fortunate in keeping one another, neither of us - none of us - escaped what happened to our home unscathed by loss and memory."

"We are not here to debate who has suffered the greatest loss," Paeral broke in before Altoneir could respond. "We are here to bring you to your new home, Altoneir. End this forced solitude and come back where you belong, where you will be welcomed and cared for, where you can once again ply your craft and create beauty."

The words were clearly meant to be seductive; Paeral and Inaadi could not see that, though his cart was filled with ordinary supplies, his pack held the gemstones and metal he would need to practice his profession right where they stood.

In the space of a heartbeat, Altoneir debated his response to the male and female before him, who at least had the foresight not to join hands while they spoke to him. Though he and Paeral had never been friendly and his relationship with Inaadi had never been more than the acquaintanceship borne of her friendship with his mate, he detected no sarcasm, no attempts to bait him. It seemed Paeral and Inaadi truly wanted him to return to Caalenor with them, and he could sense no ulterior motive.

"We have horses picketed in the grasses," Inaadi pressed, smiling softly. "They will carry us swiftly to Caalenor, just as they carried Paeral and I here. The horsemaster held enough hope for your return that she sent us with a stallion for you as well."

Altoneir directed his words at Inaadi, for it was she who had always shown him kindness, not her mate. "Thank you," he said, and found he meant it. "But I choose to remain in solitude."

"Come, Altoneir," Paeral wheedled, a slight bit of the superior note he had always used when addressing Altoneir creeping into his voice. "You know Aenwyn - "

Altoneir's magic jumped abruptly into his hands again, and both Paeral and Inaadi looked startled by the red aura of battle that immediately surrounded him. "Do not," he said with deadly quiet, "speak to me of Aenwyn. Do not let her name pass your lips for as long as you exist."

Paeral seemed to be preparing to call magic of his own, but Inaadi laid a calming hand on his shoulder. "Come, Paeral," she said, and somewhere inside his rage-filled mind, Altoneir noted she had not called him any of the affectionate names he knew they had for one another. It did nothing to calm him as she continued, "Our friend has made his position and desires clear. Let us go."

Paeral took a deep breath before nodding at his mate, avoiding Altoneir's eyes and the obvious threat he still posed.

"If you change your mind," Inaadi said softly, placatingly, looking past the aura of magic and into eyes Altoneir knew still revealed the agony he felt at the thought of his lost mate, "you must come to us. There will be a place in Caalenor waiting for you whenever you should wish it."

Paeral took her elbow then, guiding her back from Altoneir, though not daring to turn his back until they had passed the edge of the clearing. Only after they had turned and disappeared into the forest did Altoneir release his magic, and he fought to remain standing as the grief washed over him once again, mingling with his rage in a deadly cocktail of desolation and fury.

Only when Altoneir had calmed did he realize the truth of the situation, and it threatened to send him into a fury greater even than the one Paeral had caused when he had invoked Aenwyn's name. Paeral and Inaadi had not left at all...they had simply gone into the cover of the trees and cloaked themselves so he could not see them. He could feel the glamour from over a hundred feet away.

Again, Altoneir took a heartbeat to consider his response, though murdering them for the deception sounded quite appealing. Reason got the better of him, however, when he realized the fury he would bring upon himself for killing two of his own kind. So instead of casting his magic toward where he now knew they stood watching him, he feigned ignorance and show them he meant what he said about living in solitude.

Before he had even unburdened the cart still lying unattended, before he unlaced his pack to organize his new supplies, Altoneir began to gather stones to build his home, and he did not stop until he sensed, finally, that they were gone.

IANTRIS

The roundhouse in the clearing was so heavily warded that no one, not even another elf, could pass through the invisible walls surrounding it without Altoneir's leave. He liked it that way; the clearing had become a peaceful place, a home where he could work, rest, and revel in memories on his own terms.

As he tended the small kitchen garden in front of his house early one fall morning, Altoneir allowed himself the pleasure of remembering Aenwyn in their garden, humming tunelessly as she often had while she worked. He hummed like she had as he harvested the purple carrots he had planted midsummer, looking forward to their crunchy sweetness in his evening meal.

Altoneir looked at the one-stall stable he had built two years after he had first moved into the forest clearing and the horse picketed outside. Recognizing the necessity of a travel animal, Altoneir had purchased her from the human town of Bergefort once he had made enough money selling his jewels to both dwarves and humans. Folyn, as he had renamed her once she became his, ate her oat feed tranquilly this morning, content to remain idle for the time being. He knew, however, that she would not remain happy for long. It had been three days since he had taken her for a ride, and she was not a lazy beast -

she would want to go out again soon and would grow restless if he didn't take her.

Altoneir pulled a particularly well-situated root from the ground, thinking about something he had been considering for years but had never done: visiting Caalenor. His purpose, whatever it might have been in the time immediately following the avalanche, was not to see any particular elves or to consider rebuilding his life there after all the years that had passed, but to acquire some of the reading materials that had been lost when his home had been destroyed. Though he was content enough to grow his vegetables and ply his craft, only leaving his home when it was necessary to sell his goods or buy more supplies, he missed some of the tomes he had owned in Shaamel. He longed to lose himself once again in the elven epics, to see the thick book that comprised the elven dictionary on his shelves, and to find new texts to read as well. Though he had purchased a few rough copies of epic poetry in Bergefort, reading them in the poorly translated common tongue did not satisfy him in the same way as reading the flowing words in the elven tongue would have, and the taint of the human hands that had copied and translated them took away much of what value they had.

Having harvested the last of the carrot crop, Altoneir stood and dusted the soil from his hands, collecting the root vegetables to take to the stream for washing before he began setting some aside for immediate enjoyment and preserving others for winter.

After many trips to Kol Todur, several trips to the human city of Bergefort, and one memorable trip to Gelrhia in the years since he had claimed the clearing as his home, Altoneir's roundhouse and the surrounding area were as well-appointed and supplied as any home he could have wished for. Though the early times had often found him wanting one thing or another, he rarely had a moment these days in which he wished for a tool, object, or ingredient he didn't have. After the initial profit he had made with the supplies he bought on that first trip into the dwarven mining city, he had found, once again, his jewelcrafting to be a profession that could sustain him in the style he wished.

Altoneir placed the carrots in a gathering bag and left the clearing for the small but strong stream that flowed through the forest not even a mile from his home. He clicked his tongue at Folyn as he left, promising her in his own way that she would roam the trails and perhaps even the valley that day.

When he reached the stream, the path to it well-trod and as familiar as his own home, he let himself delve deeply into his own desires while he carried out the rote task of washing the soil from the vegetables and his own hands. The idea of visiting Caalenor had become more pervasive lately, but he knew he could not leave now. The round trip would take several weeks, even on Folyn's back, and the early winter of the high mountains would have set in by the time he reached the city.

Altoneir shuddered slightly at the thought of winter high in the mountains. His home was barely in the Gray Hills themselves, and though he did experience winter, it was much milder than that of the elven settlements in the Guilnora and Chilpar mountain ranges. Though his nightmares had abated somewhat in the intervening years, Altoneir did not think he could ever bear experiencing another such winter with the snow looming threateningly around him.

Spring. I'll go to Caalenor in the spring.

That decision made, Altoneir repacked the clean carrots into his bag and strode through the forest back to his home. He would take Folyn for a ride in the nearby valley but not roam far enough to reach even the closest human village, and then he would spend the afternoon working on a piece that had been commissioned by a human noble the last time he had visited Bergefort.

What she wanted was ornate and would be beautiful when complete: a small diadem with a blue stone centerpiece, surrounded by cresting waves of silver flecked with tiny glittering gems to make it shimmer. She was willing to pay handsomely for his work, wanting it as a gift for her daughter before she traveled to the royal city of Emelle to find a suitable husband, but he still felt the distaste he always felt when dealing with humans.

Altoneir had been careful never to show the rage that wanted to destroy humankind in Bergefort; he needed the business of both the nobles and the traveling merchants who converged there, and to make himself feared and reviled there would have been folly. He knew no one connected the reasoned, businesslike elf he presented himself to be with the one who terrorized the village in the valley. But he had returned to Faehill twice in the first five years after his first visit, burning and killing each time, reveling in the fear they had for his power and the rightness of the justice he was exacting upon them. When he had returned for the third time, he had found the village deserted, the human homes he had burned never having been rebuilt. They had fled him, and though it meant he would never have the pleasure of his revenge upon him again, that he had made an entire village flee had given him a sense of righteous power he never been able to duplicate. After visiting the roundhouse he had shared with Aenwyn one last time and thinking about, but ultimately rejecting the idea of moving his home to the deserted village, Altoneir had spent an entire day destroying every structure left. By the time he remounted Folyn and turned back toward his home in the Gray Hills, nothing had been left of the former settlement of Y'Sathemar.

Though he was surprised to have received no further visits from Caalenor after his deeds against the humans of the valley, he had surmised that they either did not know what he had done, or that those in power felt his retribution to be well-placed. Though he knew the reason was likely the former, he preferred to think that others agreed with him, even though they did not act as he had. He found he didn't want even elven company; the idea of sharing his life after all this time was abhorrent and terrifying in its very implications. He also knew the very treaty he loathed, the very treaty he raged against, also protected and isolated him: except for the healers in Isasari, the elves in the mountains rarely interfered in human affairs. Whatever they might have thought and felt about what he had done to Faehill and its inhabitants, they had not come.

Once Y'Sathemar was gone and the humans there scattered throughout the valley, Altoneir did not search for another village or settlement on which to exact his revenge; though the rage at what they humans had done when they had convinced the ancient elves to sign that treaty had not abated, and though Altoneir still blamed their greed for the tragedy of Shaamel, he knew beyond any doubt that continued expression of his unhappiness would bring a greater force down upon him than he could handle. He had become a nightmarish legend in Faehill, but while he still relished what he had done there, he knew he would be hunted if he did just as he wished.

Shaking himself out of the thoughts and memories, Altoneir set about his day - a day not unlike all the others preceding it, and a day that brought him peace if not joy.

ALTONEIR DISLIKED WINTER, even the more moderate one he experienced at his home in the foothills of the Gray Hills. When the snow covered his clearing in a white blanket, he often found himself glancing anxiously upward toward the mountain range to his east, as though he would soon see a wall of snow coming for him at last. It was easy to tell himself that wouldn't happen, but not so easy to banish the leftover fear from a decade before.

During the winter, his nightmares, which had all but abated in other seasons, returned full force. He couldn't view snow without seeing Aenwyn's dead face, frozen in place, her mouth and nostrils packed with snow. He couldn't view snow without remembering unearthing his parents from their home in Shaamel, and how they had held each other in death. He woke in the winter nights as often as not, either panting from his visions of his loved ones or remembering being thrown down the mountain by the force of the avalanche.

As was his habit, Altoneir stoked his fire into a hearty blaze as soon as he woke, warming his solitary roundhouse to the point at which he would hardly notice the chill of the winter air outside. His daily routine, unaltered for years, consisted of making himself his morning tea and wheat mush sweetened with whatever he had on hand, neatening his space as much as was necessary, and either reading the paltry reading material he had accumulated over the years or scratching his own quill over clean parchment, attempting his own epic poem.

He had barely finished breaking his fast when he heard something outside that should not have been there: a voice, female, calling for aid and close enough to the house that he knew she had somehow crossed the invisible barriers set by his wards. Frowning, he stood, leaving his dishes to be scrubbed after he had found the source of the disturbance.

He opened his door to find a lone elven woman robed in white even brighter than the snow surrounding her. She stood near the middle of his clearing, in danger of inadvertently stepping into the depressed pit he used for outdoor fires in the warmer months. It was almost as though she knew what he had tried to emulate in his placement of the fire pit: an elven community circle.

"Who are you?" he asked, his voice not accusatory even as he silently checked his wards, wondering how she had gotten through without so much as alerting him.

"I am called Iantris," she said, her voice soft now that she had his attention. "Forgive me for disturbing you, but I am lost. When I saw the smoke from your fire..." she trailed off, looking at him pleadingly.

Altoneir said nothing for several moments, simply surveying the elf in front of him. She was undeniably beautiful, perhaps the most beautiful female he had ever seen, other than his mate. Her long hair fell in dark curls past her shoulders, contrasting with the preternaturally pale skin that told him she had spent little time out of doors. As she gazed at him, something like a plea in her eyes, he found himself almost lost in their deep blue irises, so dark he knew they would appear black in any light lower than the bright light of the morning in a snowy clearing. As he looked her over, he noticed she was delicately shivering, her clothing not sufficient for the biting cold of the winter morning.

For a moment, Altoneir debated turning her away. He had chosen the solitude in which he lived, and even if the elf woman was beautiful, he had no wish to share his home with anyone, even temporarily.

The woman, Iantris, suddenly smiled at him, revealing perfectly white, straight teeth under her full red lips. Like the rest of her, the smile was beautiful, but that wasn't what caught Altoneir's attention. With her smile came the sudden awareness that this woman wasn't a helpless, lost elf. She was dangerous, perhaps in the same way he, himself, was dangerous. In the faintly amused curve of her lips and the gleaming white of her teeth, he saw a predator. Though he feared no danger to himself, it was at that realization that he allowed her inside his warm roundhouse. Something about her called to him as like calls to like; something about her answered a question he had not realized he had asked.

Shaking himself slightly, he smiled - letting some of the predatory nature of his own personality show. "Do come inside and get warm," he invited, his voice surprising him as it came out in a deep, seductive purr. As she gracefully strode toward the door, almost seeming to tread on the surface of the snow rather than sinking into it, he wondered why he had spoken to her in that way; he certainly couldn't recall using that tone even once in the ten years since Aenwyn had died.

"You are too kind," Iantris murmured as she crossed the threshold into the warm, dry interior of the house.

"My lady," Altoneir said, again surprising himself as he addressed her thus, "you are not garbed for the weather. How is it you have survived the winter thus far with no cloak and, it seems, no supplies?" For he had indeed noticed that she carried nothing with her - and as far away as he lived from the settled areas either of the mountains or the valley, she should not have been able to reach him without warm clothing and a full pack.

"My supplies were taken as I slept," Iantris told him, taking a seat without being invited into one of the two carved wooden chairs Altoneir had brought from his trip to Gelrhia years before. "I detected no thieves and yet awoke with nothing but the clothing on my back." She indicated the white robes, which, while not exactly thin, were not suitable for winter travel. At least, Altoneir noticed, she wore black leather traveling boots lined with gray fur.

"Most mysterious," was all he said in response to her claim, though he was uncertain he believed what she had told him. No one should have been able to take everything she had down, it seemed, to the blankets she would have been sleeping in, without waking her. Deciding not to challenge her just yet, he waited to hear what else she had to say. Though he couldn't explain why, he felt a pull to help her rather than to question her. Clearly, she had crossed his path for a reason.

Iantris didn't address her appearance again; instead, she looked around his well-appointed roundhouse with interest as she held her hands out to the fire. "You live as the elves in Caalenor do," she commented, surveying the belongings he had accumulated over the years. Her eyes rested on a blue vase of blown glass, which had purchased from a dwarven artisan just months before.

"Though I like my solitude, lady, I enjoy the same accoutrements of my kind," he said smoothly. "Why should it be unexpected that I live as other elves do?"

She pursed her lips. "Many of your belongings are of dwarf make," she commented. "You seem to not have communed with our kind in quite some time, perhaps since you have lived in this place." She stood, dropping her hands to her side, and glided over to the shelf that held the two dozen or so scrolls he had accumulated. Without asking leave, she picked up the topmost one and unfurled it, examining the words within.

"The tale is of our kind," she mused, "but this is written in the common tongue. Why have you a translation rather than a copy in its original language?"

Somewhere outside himself, Altoneir knew he would have bristled at the prying question had anyone else asked it, but nothing about this woman irritated him. In fact, her interest was flattering; after so many years of solitude, it was pleasant to have someone show interest in how and where he lived. "I have not returned to elven lands in over ten years," he said. "Though I intend to visit Caalenor in the spring, until that time I must make do with what I can attain from the human and dwarven settlements closest to me." He thought of Folyn, warm in her straw-lined stable, and knew his words weren't precisely true. He could have traveled with ease to any number of elven settlements, including Isasari in the valley.

Iantris seemed to hear the untruth in his voice, for she pursed her lips again. "You have avoided our kind in favor of dwarves and humans," she stated, her tone gentle but firm. "Do you prefer those races to ours?"

Altoneir chuckled, the sound sardonic against the merry crackling of his fire. "I absolutely do not," he answered. "I find dwarves irritating at best, and humans reprehensible."

Iantris nodded, as though his answer confirmed what she had suspected all along. "You avoid our kind because you do not wish to remember," she breathed, her gaze hooded as she leveled it at him. "You do not wish to remember that which you have lost."

Altoneir said nothing. How had she been able to glean that from their brief conversation thus far? He suddenly had the feeling this woman knew him much better than she should have, considering he had never seen her before in his life.

Taking his silence as confirmation, she stepped closer to him, standing not a foot away. "It is time to remember," she said, her voice intense but low. "It is time to remember, and it is time to right the imbalance in the world."

FOR THE FIRST time in ten years, Altoneir told his story in full: the avalanche in Shaamel and the horrors that still plagued him, his grief for his lost mate, and the retribution he had taken against some of the humans in the valley for being the cause of their sorrow. He told her of his hatred for the necessary relationship between himself and the humans of Bergefort and of how he took some satisfaction in making sure he got the better end of every transaction he had with them. He told her of the peace of his home in the clearing and the pleasure he had found in plying his craft and caring for himself.

For a full day and into the night, he had talked with little interruption from Iantris other than the occasional clarifying question. And he wasn't sure why, but he knew none of what he told her caused her to think less of him: not the continued nightmares and fear, not the rage, and not even his messy retribution on Faehill when they had denied him a piece of their safety and security in his old home.

When he reached the part of his tale in which he had gone back to Faehill to find it deserted, Iantris actually nodded in satisfaction, seeming to find the same sense of rightness in their flight as he had. Again, the predator behind her beautiful face revealed itself, almost seeming to glow in the elven light he had set in the roundhouse. It was that moment at which Altoneir knew she felt the same way about humans as he did; it was that moment at which he realized that she might have known about his actions before she had come to his home and sought him out for that very reason.

Storing the realization for further consideration later, Altoneir continued his tale, not stopping until the wee hours of the morning. And when he finally stopped, finally spent of the words and the confessions he had laid at her feet, she came to him.

Altoneir felt separate from his own body the first time he touched her, as though he was looking down at himself from a distant corner of the room. He hadn't imagined touching anyone else the way he had once touched Aenwyn — he hadn't ever contemplated that he might take another lover, much less another mate, once she was gone from his life. And yet, there was his hand, cupping her perfectly smooth cheek in a lover's caress...there was his mouth on hers...

He woke late the next morning to find her still sleeping, her legs tangled in his under the furs and blankets of the bed he had never shared. For a few moments, he just looked at her, watching her sleep as he had once watched Aenwyn sleep. Iantris's face was not as peaceful in repose as Aenwyn's was, and he reached with one long finger to touch the tiny furrow between her eyes, as though she were deep in contemplation even as she slept.

She stirred, opening her eyes to gaze upon him. The small furrow disappeared, leaving her forehead as smooth and pale as the blanket of snow outside.

Altoneir did not smile as he continued to gaze at her and did not speak any of the morning endearments he had shared with his mate. He simply wondered who this woman was and how she had ended up in his lonely bed…for he realized now just how lonely he had been. In the guise of peace, in the effort not to have to relive the grief of Shaamel with others, he had isolated himself for over a decade. He wondered if it had been fate that had led her to his clearing; he wondered if it had been chance that had led her to seek his help.

Though he had provided her with food, shelter, and even one of his fur-lined cloaks, Altoneir felt in that moment that she had given him so much more. She had listened to his tale, and telling it had not been the traumatic experience he had expected it to be; rather, he had found it to be a cleansing experience, as though giving that piece of himself to another was the next step in moving forward to the life he was meant to live. She had given him a sense of belonging, even after only being with him for two days, that he hadn't felt since leaving his mountainside home. And their lovemaking…

Altoneir blew out a breath. He felt their lovemaking the night before had been the beginning of something, but of what he could not tell. He was certainly not interested in having another mate, not that he would have considered such a step with one he had only just met, anyway. But he thought that, even without the lifetime commitment he had shared with Aenwyn, he would enjoy her company for a long while yet.

"Good morning," Iantris said, her voice breathy with sleep.

Altoneir, as though guided by a hand he couldn't see, kissed her smooth brow. "Good morning," he answered. Without saying another word, he got out of bed, cursing internally at the cold winter air on his naked body. Crossing to the fireplace, he used his magic to start the blaze up from the embers that had died while they slept.

He looked back at the bed where Iantris still lay, the furs gathered close around her. "How soon must you depart?" he asked, somehow dreading the answer. If she were to leave as suddenly as she had appeared, he knew the clearing and his home would seem much emptier than they had before she had come. He found, to his surprise, that he didn't want her to leave; something about her called to him in a way he couldn't explain, a pull that should not have existed.

Iantris tilted her head to one side, studying him and seeming to consider his question. "I have some time yet," she said. "My plans cannot be carried out until spring." Altoneir waited for a few moments, but decided not to question her when she wasn't forthcoming about her plans. Dimly, he realized he *should* question her, but something about the way she had said the words, the way she looked at him, had made him unwilling to do so.

He pulled his green woolen robes from the peg on the wall and dressed himself, the fabric feeling rough on a body that suddenly seemed more physically sensitive than it had for a long while.

Iantris still made no move to get dressed; having refused to wear a set of his robes, she had instead opted to wash hers at his stream the day before, breaking the ice to get to the freezing water beneath, and had seemed somewhat awed when he dried them with a waft of summer-warm air. The white robes now lay in a pile beside the bed, right where they had been left when she had stripped for him the night before. She ignored them as she watched him dress, her eyes hungry for more of what they had shared.

After he had pulled on his robes, a set of woolen socks, and his winter boots, Altoneir left her behind as he ventured into the room he had not shown her yet, the adjoining, circular room that held his worktable and his jewelcrafting supplies. Ignoring the works-in-progress neatly arranged on his table, Altoneir crossed the room to the wooden strongbox where he kept finished pieces for sale, each displayed on a velvet cushion of its own.

Altoneir immediately spotted the one he had been looking for: the largest saltwater pearl he had ever seen, bought from a trader in Bergefort who had bought it from a merchant from the seaside city of Saltmire. As had the dwarven diamond so many years before, the pearl had caught his eye and he had purchased it without knowing what its purpose would be. Bringing it home, he had set it with a triad of small diamonds on a gold chain that resembled a thin, smooth rope. Knowing the simplicity of the setting and chain would allow the large, almost-perfect sphere to compliment whomever wore it, Altoneir had set the piece aside to sell during his spring trip to Caalenor - he knew many elves would find the deceptive simplicity of the piece enchanting.

Now, however, he knew he would give the piece away rather than selling it in Caalenor. The idea did not give him the least bit of pause, for of course he should grace the one who shared his bed with such a gift; he knew it with a certainty he didn't entirely understand, but he acted upon it, nonetheless. He carried it back into the main room and over to the bed, where Iantris still reclined under the furs. Wordlessly, he took her hand, turned it palm-up, and placed the necklace into it. "For you," he said unnecessarily, his voice a husky almost-growl he didn't recognize from himself.

Perhaps desire is addling my mind.

Iantris sat up, letting the fur fall around her, exposing her bare chest in the now-warm room. Gazing down at the jewel in her hand, her face held less of the astonished gratitude he had expected and hoped for, and more a sense of entitlement.

Why should she not feel that way? Has she not brought me from my isolation back into life?

"Thank you," Iantris said, immediately fastening the necklace around her slim, pale neck. It fell just beneath her throat, the pearl casting an opalescent glow as it reflected the fire. "It is beautiful, more beautiful than anything I have seen in many years."

"No, my lady. The thanks are due to you," Altoneir said, still in that husky voice, "and the pearl was only waiting for you to come."

HUNTERS

"**D**o you remember the terms under which the treaty between elves and humans was made?" Iantris asked Altoneir one late winter day as he painstakingly worked over an uncut gemstone he had bought from the dwarves in Kol Todur the summer prior. The stone was the deep red of blood, a ruby so brilliantly colored he thought the very essence of it symbolized hatred and violence.

To make this into a thing of beauty, he thought, *is to shape that very hatred into something one would pay to possess.* He already knew the finished piece would be something he would hold for a visit to the human cities, rather than Caalenor or Gelrhia; only humans would want to purchase something created so. As he painstakingly crafted it, he channeled his hatred into the gem, his will and his power, to make it into an object that would unwittingly reveal the ugliness of whomever wore it.

Using the tiniest blade of magic to shave a sliver of the gem onto the small waste pile atop his table, Altoneir did not glance up at Iantris as he answered her. "Of course," he said absently, looking for the correct placement for the next cut. "Though I was not present at the negotiations, not being a diplomat myself, I well remember being presented with the terms even as we were ordered to abandon Y'Sathemar." He scowled at the memory; he had not been the only elf of Y'Sathemar who had resented and resisted the order. His own father, Ayduin, had spent several days outright refusing to leave their home and all they had built there. In the end, however, the might of the ancient elders of Caalenor gave them no choice; they would leave, or they would face consequences great enough to end their entire settlement.

"It was thought the elves, who are hardier than humans, of course, would survive more fruitfully on the mountain than the new race would. It was thought that the conditions on the mountain would be too harsh for their fragile, mortal bodies."

Altoneir looked up at her words, gazing into her eyes, black this morning without the reflection of the sun and snow outside. "So it was thought," he agreed. "And not without much careful plotting and prodding from the human emissaries. Given how their race has multiplied since their arrival here, I find them rather more able to survive than they portrayed themselves to be in the early days."

"You lived in the settlement of Y'Sathemar," Iantris mused. "And were forced to leave your home when the treaty was signed. Thus, you founded the settlement of Shaamel in the Chilpar Mountains."

Altoneir turned back to the gemstone; though he was never exactly impatient with Iantris, he felt that her prodding this morning was repetitive. They had already gone over the elves' exile from Y'Sathemar several times, including when he had individually been forbidden to live there a decade before. The subject did nothing but rekindle the rage he worked so hard to suppress; it never brought him peace. Sometimes, in the darkness when Iantris lay sleeping beside him, he wondered if she was kindling his rage for some purpose of her own. He found he didn't care if she was.

He made another cut, creating a new facet through which the inner glow of the ruby, reflected from the firelight across the room, was put on full display.

"Fire and blood," Altoneir murmured.

Iantris came to peer over his shoulder as he made another magical cut, the removed sliver of gemstone so small it was hardly visible as it fell to join the others in the waste pile. Altoneir never shared his technique with anyone, but he truly felt that to create jewels that seemed to sparkle with their own light, the smaller, shaved cuts were far more important than the larger ones.

Altoneir didn't mind as she silently watched him make another cut, this one slightly larger, producing a flake rather than a sliver of the ruby. "Fire and blood," she said, her voice strong as he used his cloth to polish the spot he had just cut.

Altoneir put the ruby down and turned to face her; he realized she had something on her mind. He looked at her questioningly and with the same patience he had used to grant only to Aenwyn when she interrupted his work. "You have something to tell me," he stated matter-of-factly.

"Does it not occur to you that these greedy, self-serving people now have the rule over much of Ilbeor? When they came, they were small in numbers and populated only about half the valley they so successfully negotiated for as our ancient elders sought to avoid a war over territory. Now, they stand as the largest race of the land and occupy the land to match those numbers. Why, they have broken the treaty themselves, though of course they do not see it as such."

Altoneir lost interest in the gem he had been so carefully cutting. "Come," he said quietly, aware this conversation was about to take a more important turn than others before it. "Sit with me."

As they moved into the roundhouse's main room, Altoneir noted that, while nothing had physically changed about the space since Iantris occupied it, the very essence seemed different, somehow full of her presence even if she had brought no belongings and made no alterations.

Iantris did not immediately make for the small sitting area in front of the fire; instead, she removed the teapot from the trivet, where she had obviously placed it to boil before seeking him out.

She knew I would stop for this discussion.

He sat down in his usual chair, absently smoothing his winter robes over his lap as he waited for her to pour steaming water over the prepared tea leaves in two ceramic mugs. She had chosen nettle tea for this winter's afternoon, and the slightly bitter, piney scent of it filled his nostrils as it steeped.

Only when she had handed Altoneir his mug and sat down across from him did Iantris speak again. "Do you ever wonder why the humans may live on their royal mountain, though the treaty specifically states the mountains in the north to be elven territory? Do you know why the ancient kings moved from their island to rule from that place?"

"I do not," Altoneir replied, sipping the scalding hot tea carefully. It was the truth, as was the fact that he had never given the matter much thought. No one had inhabited what was now the human's royal mountain in all of Ilbeor's history, at least that he knew of. Most of elvenkind considered it far too remote for their dealings with one another and the other races.

"The human king at the time brought himself to Caalenor along with his entourage and stated that, unless the treaty was amended to allow them to dwell there, they - the humans, in their greater numbers - would wage war on our kind. And though our magic makes us formidable in battle, their sheer numbers would have meant heavy losses to ensure victory. The elders of Caalenor believed, and still believe, that ceding this territory to the humans was superior to engaging in open war."

Altoneir did not speak. He had never been aware of the details of the arrangement; had never known it had come about because the humans had threatened open war. Thinking of it now, he thought it had been wise of the elders to keep that detail from becoming common knowledge; enough elves resented the humans' seizure of the fertile valley that some might have thought meeting them in battle superior to ceding any more land, even if it was uninhabited.

"The humans took their prize without having to strive or fight for it," Iantris continued, her voice becoming harder than Altoneir had ever heard. "Our elders simply looked at their greater numbers and made the concession, and you see what has come of it."

Altoneir nodded, the picture forming wholly in his head as though it had always been there. Humans had taken possession of the royal mountain and, with it, had expanded both their territory and their influence from the southern to the northern borders of the continent.

"No other race holds a place in their council chambers," Iantris continued inexorably, as though she had wanted to discuss this with him since the very beginning. "Certainly not the elves, their closest neighbors. But they also exclude the dwarves, tselqs, and twanai from their machinations. They rule over the greatest swath of land in Ilbeor, and they share that rule with no one."

Before Altoneir could respond, she stood and dusted her hands as though wiping them clean of the information and insinuations she had just shared with him. "I must walk," she declared, taking the fur-lined cloak he had given her from its peg by the door. She did not invite him to come; in fact, she did not even wait for his acknowledgement before she disappeared into the snow.

WITH SOME DIFFICULTY, Altoneir returned to his work on the blood ruby after it became clear Iantris wasn't planning to return for some time. As the facets gleamed under his skilled hands as though there was fire within the stone, Altoneir thought more about what she had said.

His rage had been justified, and her explanation of the humans' machinations with the treaty and the subsequent expansion of their territory only convinced him more wholly than he had ever been that it had been human greed and hubris that had caused Shaamel's destruction.

It wasn't until he was polishing the finished gem he could finally let go of his absolute control over his movements, and he found that as he buffed the facets of the knuckle-sized stone, his hand moved faster and faster until the polishing cloth became a blur of motion. He had thought his rage had ebbed...he had thought that he might be on the road to tolerance with the humans in the valley...he had thought wrong.

Hardier indeed, he thought savagely. No amount of hardiness would have allowed Aenwyn to survive the avalanche any more than the humans would have. The humans had fooled the elders into thinking they would only be safe in the valley, and they had done it at the expense of the elves forced into the mountains. Shaamel was the result of their wickedness...Shaamel was the result of elven short-sightedness in pursuing peace with the newly arrived race.

By the time Iantris returned as the day was falling into the gloom of winter twilight, the finished gem lay gleaming on Altoneir's worktable, and he sat in his chair before the fire again, a glass of liquor in one long-fingered hand.

Iantris stamped the snow from her boots before she entered the roundhouse, taking off her cloak and hanging it again on the peg by the door. Without saying a word, she crossed to Altoneir and kissed his brow before sinking into the chair next to his. But for the falling dark outside, they looked almost as though they had not moved from their positions earlier that day, as though the conversation would continue with no interruption.

They sat in silence for several long moments, Altoneir finishing his glass of red liquor as Iantris warmed her hands by the fire. Then Iantris, as though she couldn't allow the silence to go on any longer, said, "Your actions against the humans of Faehill were justified, my love, but stop now to reflect: were they enough?"

Altoneir looked at her, startled out of his reverie both by her use of the endearment he hadn't heard in so many years, and by her statement. "We cannot just roam the valley, slaughtering as we go," he said calmly, as though what she had suggested was reasonable if flawed. "Caalenor would never stand for it, much less the humans. There are only two of us..." He trailed off as Iantris leaned forward, placing her forearms on her knees as she gazed at him.

"No amount of slaughter you or I could accomplish on our own would be half enough to exact payment for what they have taken from us," she said, her voice brittle. For the first time since they had met, she seemed to be showing the same rage he, himself, felt.

"Then what else is to be done?" Altoneir asked. He had a sudden feeling of destiny descending upon him, a feeling of momentousness he couldn't explain.

"There is an island," Iantris said, her voice suddenly a harsh whisper, as though she feared the very world would be listening to her words. "The very island the humans once ruled from, actually. They named it Sundersar, after one of their ancient kings. It sits abandoned now, a fortress atop its tallest hill…"

Altoneir listened, entranced, while she wove for him a picture of elvendom again taking the rulership of Ilbeor, of humans being forced back into their natural place, even of the other three races gaining more influence in the land.

"You have a chance, beloved," she said softly when she was finished, "to not only bring Ilbeor back under the rule of the more reasoned, intelligent race for the betterment of all…but to take that rule for yourself."

Altoneir's mind went back to the blood-red ruby lying on the table, undoubtedly glowing with the embers of the fire he had stopped tending when his work was done. Fire and blood…cunning and might rather than ill-tempered rage. If Iantris was right, together they could bring Ilbeor to its knees.

ALTONEIR RODE to Bergefort without Iantris once winter had thawed into an early spring; he needed supplies and had several finished pieces to sell to the nobility, many of whom would be preparing to spend the summer season in Emelle grasping for favorable marriages and other alliances among the houses.

As Folyn trod the familiar streets to the only inn Altoneir could tolerate, an upscale place meant for wealthy merchants and minor nobility, he had trouble keeping his face neutral. Now, after spending most of the winter making plans with Iantris, the humans seemed more reprehensible to him than they ever had. How they strutted about the streets, especially the wealthy. How they haggled with him as though they could ever find the equal of his work among their own kind. How they grasped for favor, for any kind of edge over those they called their friends.

Disgusting.

He had no trouble selling the pieces he had made, particularly the blood ruby, which he had set into a tiara of swirling gold. Several merchants had made competing offers for it, believing they could sell it for a formidable profit in the city of Emelle itself, but they had all lost out to a noblewoman who had offered twice their highest bid. As Altoneir made the exchange, he had to work to keep the utter disdain from his face as he read her obvious greed. *She did not buy the piece for its beauty*, he concluded. *She bought it to show her own wealth. So typical, so very typical.*

Still, he pocketed the money for the tiara and several smaller pieces besides and, after spending only two nights in the inn, made his way back to the clearing and Iantris. She had not left his side from the moment of her arrival in early winter until his departure for Bergefort, but she had balked from visiting the bustling town with him, pointing out that he had only one horse. He was looking forward to seeing her again with a fervor that surprised him, and as he rode, he wondered, not for the first time, at the hold she seemed to have on him.

As he reached his home of almost eleven years, he stopped short just outside of his clearing, for there, sitting astride horses directly in his path, sat Paeral and Inaadi.

"Greetings, Altoneir," Paeral said, and his voice held none of the wheedling compassion it had when he had visited before. No, this voice was a voice meant to show some kind of authority Paeral thought he had gained in the intervening years; this voice was the voice of an elf who wanted to compel him to action.

"Paeral. Inaadi."

"Ten years have passed, and we have come to bring you home at last," Paeral said, his tone brokering no arguments.

"We could not pass into the clearing," Inaadi said with a small smile. "We thought we would have to wait for you to come out; as it turns out, we waited for you to come in."

"I see you have found a new mate," Paeral said, his tone sharp. "After only ten years? Altoneir, I'm surprised - "

"She is not my mate," Altoneir cut in. "She has been a friend to me, and nothing more." He resented the implication that he would have moved on from Aenwyn, that he would have *replaced* her. He would never take another mate so long as he continued to exist.

"Perhaps your new 'friend' will join us in Caalenor," Paeral said smoothly. "Perhaps she will enjoy the city."

"I will not be accompanying you to Caalenor," Altoneir said through gritted teeth. Never mind any plans he and Iantris had made, he had never had any plans to return to the elven city for anything more than a visit.

"You will," Paeral insisted. "Or we will be forced to - "

"Forced to what, exactly? I live a peaceful existence here."

"We have heard differently," Inaadi cut in softly. "For the last five years, Caalenor has housed a contingent of humans while their surveyors searched for a safe place to establish a new village."

"They sought our protection from *you*," Paeral said, his voice acid. "They have lived among us these five years, but now that they have found a plot of land suitable for their village and got royal permission to build, they find themselves afraid to leave the confines of Caalenor."

"The ancients have promised them you will leave the valley," Inaadi said, her voice softer that Paeral's, but still carrying a note of authority she had never used on him before. "When we heard of their plans, Paeral and I begged the chance to bring you home ourselves rather than - "

"Rather than what?" Altoneir asked sharply.

"Rather than sending a force of hunters to bring you back," Paeral answered, his tone making it perfectly clear that he did not mean game hunters, but those who enforced elven law and protected elven borders.

Altoneir's lip curled. "So, you have offered these *humans* safe harbor in your city for five years, and it is only to convince them to return to the valley that you finally seek retribution against me?" He laughed, and it was cold and bitter rather than mirthful.

"We do not seek retribution," Inaadi said, a note of pleading in her voice now. "You would face only one restriction, and that is that you would stay in Caalenor for five and twenty years. You would not be imprisoned; you would have your own home and shop - "

"No." Altoneir sneered the word, not letting her finish her plea. "I have no wish to live among elves who would offer asylum to humans. I have no wish to live among a people who pander peace over the protection of their own kind."

"Perhaps if you had extended that same passion to protecting your own mate, we would not be standing here."

Altoneir barely heard Inaadi's soft gasp of horror as Paeral finished speaking the words she knew had damned them both. Before a conscious thought had even entered his mind, he had flung his most destructive magic at both of them, throwing them off their horses and onto the ground, muddy from the spring thaw. Dismounting Folyn at last, he stalked over to them, his boots pounding into the mud with all the force of the hatred in his heart.

He was pleased that Inaadi was already gone; it would have been quick and almost painless as his magical bolt had shot through her heart. Paeral, however, he had struck in the gut, and purposefully so.

The male lay gasping on the ground, his hand extended to his dead mate, opening and closing it in a vain attempt to touch her one last time.

Altoneir did not allow it, would not allow him even the small comfort of touching her before he died. With hardly a glance at him, he summoned the death-flame and set her body ablaze. Within moments, it was gone, and Altoneir took no small amount of pleasure in the raw devastation on Paeral's face as his mate's body had disappeared into ashes on the breeze.

"Perhaps," Altoneir said, standing over him, the red battle magic once again roiling and festering between his hands, "if you had given a thought to protecting *your* mate, we would not be standing here."

The downed elf could not answer through the blood gurgling in his throat, but Altoneir saw the fear and hatred in his eyes as he reduced the magic between his hands from a ball to the fine blade he used when crafting jewelry.

Paeral couldn't even scream as Altoneir set to work.

THOUGH ALTONEIR hardly felt Paeral deserved the honor of having his body burned before the carrion eaters found it, he knew with a kind of detached certainty that he could not leave evidence of what he had done for the elven hunters to find. And as he set the death flame onto Paeral's broken and mutilated body, he felt a sense of closure he had not known he needed. Shaamel was gone, and his only way out of his grief was forward...forward for the betterment of the elven race... forward to end the hold humankind had on the land.

As he returned to the roundhouse, spattered with blood and gore and reeking of his kills, Iantris met him at the door.

Her smile of greeting was the most beautiful thing he had ever seen.

FROM THE PROPHECY OF BEIANARIAN AND THE MAGUS

Blooming petal, budding leaf, healing heart
Soft notes, home plays in musical breezes
A new life forged in the ashes of grief
Tranquility blossoms, exuding peace.
False virtue emanating purity
Offers soothing balm to a weary soul
Power yielded to deception's embrace
Poison falls as rain, cloaked in honeyed words.

Betrayed land abandoned to rank decay
Festering, stained with evils long past
Waiting for the reawakening steps
Of corrupt majesty ruling anew.
Souls flowing to the banner of evil
Unknowing the stain of promise and pledge
Slumbering land quakes in apprehension
The goddess smiles upon her borrowed throne.

Heralded saviors indeterminate
Balance and hope lost to depravity's taint

Grief fells the land, power led far astray
Silent divinity suffers the storm.

from The Prophecy of Beianarian and the Magus
set forth by Algernon of House Agelon
Second Age, 246

ACKNOWLEDGMENTS

Creation almost never takes place in a vacuum. Whether an author has a team of people helping them, as I do, or simply the support from those around them for the creative process and the demands it makes on our time, energy, and mood, it takes a lot of moving parts to make any act of creation possible.

My first thanks are always for my family, particularly my partner, Jeffrey, and my children. Without their support, understanding, and enthusiasm, even just the physical act of writing these books, the time spent at my computer, would not have been possible. And when the going gets tough and the words aren't flowing, they are inevitably the ones who lift me back up and give me the encouragement and accountability I need to work through those difficulties. I'd also like to thank my amazing mother, Cindy Mendoza, for her constant support and pride in my accomplishments. When the discouragement gets real, my mom is right there to talk me off the ledge and remind me of the value in what I'm doing and, more importantly, the joy of it.

As for the process itself – well, I could never have done it without my advance readers. Alpha readers Elle Tarragan, Crystal Darks, Finley James, and Ruby Wynn made valuable observations during the writing of *From the Sundering Snows* that helped me shape the narrative with my readers in mind. This book would not be what it is without those four amazing women. My beta readers, who received the manuscript in full, gave me valuable insight on the story as a whole: Alan Rogers, Windy Desmond, and Crystal Darks gave me not only valuable tweaks to the finished story but gave me the last bit of encouragement I needed to put it out into the world. These critical readers, who do this work for me from the goodness of their bottom-less hearts, helped me turn this story from a vague notion inside my own mind to the finished product you (hopefully) enjoyed today!

Lastly, I'd like to thank Marta and the amazing designers at getcovers.com for their service and creativity in fashioning my cover art. They've exceeded my expectations every time, and I look forward to continued partnership with them!

So to my village – both named and unnamed – thank you for your support and encouragement. I hope you're all ready, because the work isn't done!

ABOUT THE AUTHOR

T.J. Klapprodt lives and works in the vibrant city of Fort Worth, Texas, alongside her partner Jeffrey, her children Patrick and Cynthia, and her critters Finnick, Sophie, and Margie. A woman of many passions, T.J. is a dedicated teacher of newcomer emergent bilingual students, loves all things related to books and literature, and enjoys every iteration of Super Mario Brothers Nintendo has to offer.

When she is not building new fictional worlds, teaching, reading, or indulging in video games, you can find T.J. enjoying her favorite movies (usually old ones she has seen countless times), cuddling with her critters, or playing taxi driver for her children and their friends. Her family is her entire world, and she relishes nothing more than spending time at home with the ones she loves most.

T.J. graduated from Texas A&M University in 2001 with a Bachelor of Science in Psychology and from University of Texas at Arlington in 2012 with a Master of Arts in English Literature. She considers herself a lifelong learner, especially when it comes to the art of story-telling, and is always seeking to improve in her personal life, her career, and her writing.

T.J.'s greatest hope and lifelong dream is to share stories with the world, sending readers on literary adventures to ignite their imaginations, fuel their passions, and satisfy their human need for exploration, love, connection, and loss. She hopes you'll join her for this first of many forays into the world of Ilbeor!

ALSO BY T.J. KLAPPRODT

Did you enjoy *From the Sundering Snows*? Find out how Altoneir's plans come to fruition in *Messengers of Ilbeor*, available on Amazon or directly from T.J. on her website!

Want more from the *Legends of Ilbeor* saga? The next installment, *Court of the Seven Dances*, will be available in January 2025 on Amazon and directly from T.J.!

For up-to-date information and stories from T.J., along with a free Ilbeor Story for joining, subscribe to her biweekly newsletter – she promises not to spam you or share your information with anyone! Scan the QR below to get in on the journey!

Come see T.J. at www.tjklapprodt.com or contact her via email at tj@tjklapprodt.com!

www.ingramcontent.com/pod-product-compliance
Lightning Source LLC
Chambersburg PA
CBHW061545310726
48972CB00008B/2622